ANTIQUES FATE

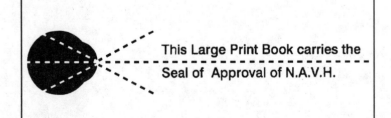

This Large Print Book carries the Seal of Approval of N.A.V.H.

A TRASH 'N' TREASURES MYSTERY

ANTIQUES FATE

BARBARA ALLAN

THORNDIKE PRESS
A part of Gale, Cengage Learning

GALE
CENGAGE Learning·

Farmington Hills, Mich • San Francisco • New York • Waterville, Maine
Meriden, Conn • Mason, Ohio • Chicago

Copyright © 2016 by Max Allan Collins and Barbara Collins.
Thorndike Press, a part of Gale, Cengage Learning.

ALL RIGHTS RESERVED
Thorndike Press® Large Print Mystery.
The text of this Large Print edition is unabridged.
Other aspects of the book may vary from the original edition.
Set in 16 pt. Plantin.

LIBRARY OF CONGRESS CATALOGING-IN-PUBLICATION DATA

Names: Allan, Barbara, author.
Title: Antiques fate : a trash 'n' treasures mystery / by Barbara Allan.
Description: Large print edition. | Waterville, Maine : Thorndike Press, 2017. |
  Series: Thorndike Press large print mystery
Identifiers: LCCN 2016050536| ISBN 9781410497642 (hardcover) | ISBN 141049764X
  (hardcover)
Subjects: LCSH: Borne, Brandy (Fictitious character)—Fiction. | Borne, Vivian
  (Fictitious character)—Fiction. | Antique dealers—Fiction. | Mothers and
  daughters—Fiction. | Murder—Investigation—Fiction. | Large type books. |
  GSAFD: Mystery fiction.
Classification: LCC PS3601.L4 A823 2017 | DDC 813/.6—dc23
LC record available at https://lccn.loc.gov/2016050536

Published in 2017 by arrangement with Kensington Books, an imprint
of Kensington Publishing Corp.

Printed in the United States of America
1 2 3 4 5 6 7 21 20 19 18 17

For Marthayn and Bob —
the write couple

Brandy's Quote:
Fate is getting a tax refund check and
finding a pair of designer shoes for that
exact amount.

— Brandy Borne

Mother's Quote:
Deep in the man sits fast his fate to
mould his fortunes, mean or great. . . .

— Ralph Waldo Emerson, *Fate*

Old York

Ye Olde Tea Room

Apothecary

Community Center

Haberdashery

Lancaster Development

Brighton Street

Cambridge Street

Manchester Street

Village Green

Red Lion Pub

The Old York Museum

London Street

Flora's Floral Shoppe

Bank

Stratford on Avon

The Horse and Groom Inn

To Serenity

New Vic Theater

Canterbury Lane

Episcopal Church

Antiques Sleuths, a new reality TV series scheduled to begin airing next summer, is set to go into production this winter in the small Iowa town of Serenity. Producing is cinematographer-turned-showrunner Phillip Dean, stepping in to replace late reality-show guru Bruce Spring (*Extreme Hobbies* and *Witch Wives of Winnipeg*).

But will shooter Dean be able to fill a show runner's gumshoes? And what motive beyond ratings instigates the new series?

Dean, contacted for evidence at his California home in Holmby Hills, said, "The premise of *Antiques Sleuths* is unique: two amateur sleuths — a mother and daughter team — who have solved a number of real-life murder mysteries in their quaint hometown — uncover the mysteries behind the strange and unusual antiques that are brought in to their shop."

Mother is Vivian Borne (age not provided), a widowed antiques dealer with a bloodhound's nose for sniffing out murder and mayhem. Daughter is Brandy Borne, a thirty-two-year-old divorcée who plays reluctant Watson to her mother's zealous

Holmes, with the help of an ever-so-cute shih tzu named Sushi.

The duo have written a number of popular books chronicling their cases under their joint pseudonym, Barbara Allan. The series, however, will not focus on their amateur detecting, but on their antiques shop.

As mysteriously intriguing as this new show may sound, this Tinseltown detective deduces that in a saturated reality TV market, the verdict may already be in: *Antiques Sleuths* risks arriving DOA.

— Rona Reed

CHAPTER ONE:
ALL THE WORLD'S A STAGE

Have you ever had a moment when everything was so perfect that you wanted to stop time?

Well, that moment was now. And now was me curled up with my boyfriend, Tony, on his couch in front of a lazy fire, the fragrantly nutty smell of hickory logs permeating the rustic cabin. The only sound was an occasional snap, crackle, and pop of the wood — with no resemblance to Rice Krispies, and with a counterpoint of light snoring from Sushi, my shih tzu, nestled on the floor next to Tony's dog, Rocky, a mixed breed mutt with a stylish black circle around one eye.

I was (and for that matter am) Brandy Borne, thirty-two, of Danish stock, a bottle-blonde with shoulder-length hair; at that moment, I was casually attired in a plaid tan and red shirt from J. Crew, my fave DKNY jeans, plus sparkly gold flats by

Toms (because a girl always needs some bling).

My BF's idea of dressing casual was a pale yellow polo shirt, tan slacks, and brown slip-on shoes sans socks. In his late forties, with graying temples, a square jaw, thick neck, and barrel chest, Tony Cassato had taken a rare day off from his job as Serenity's chief of police, and we had spent a pleasant afternoon together in his hideaway home in the country, making a midday meal, grilling steaks and fall vegetables from his garden, which we then ate on the porch in the warm autumn sunshine.

My contribution to the afternoon was to bring the dessert and, as promised, I'd made a cheesecake and conveyed it to my car. But en route I noticed the delight that I'd placed in its pan on the passenger's seat had liquefied like Vincent Price at the end of an Edgar Allan Poe movie.

In horror and disgust, I picked up the pan and pitched it and its contents out my window, flying in the face of a possible arrest by my boyfriend. (If apprehended, I would plead justifiable littering.)

What a waste of time and money! And to think, I had a perfectly good family cheesecake recipe, but no, instead I had to take one from a "healthy food" Internet site that called for low-fat cream cheese. So cheese-cake lovers everywhere, be forewarned. Ain't nothin' like the real thing, baby.

Here's what I *should* have made:

PERFECTLY GOOD CHEESECAKE
(No Health Benefits Promised)
1 graham cracker piecrust
4 pkgs. (8 oz. each) cream cheese, softened
1 cup sugar
1 tsp. vanilla
4 eggs

Beat cream cheese, sugar, and vanilla with mixer until blended. Add eggs, one at a time, mixing on low speed after each just until blended. Pour into crust. Bake one hour at 325 degrees, or until center is almost set. Cool, then refrigerate four hours.

My solution, at that moment, was to turn around, drive back into town, and buy a cheesecake at the Hy-Vee bakery, who had a pretty fair recipe themselves. I had left the evidence of the packaging in the car and, not lying really, allowed Tony to assume I'd made the excellent result.

I asked him, "So . . . what did you think of the cheesecake?"

Tony, his arm around me, said, "I loved it.

All men love cheesecake."

"I don't think I'll pursue that one."

The fire snapped and crackled and popped. Maybe next time I'd bring Krispie Treats. How can you screw that up? (Actually, you can.)

He asked offhandedly, "How's Vivian doing?"

I twisted my neck to give him a squinty look, like a pirate captain about to clobber his too-talkative first mate. "You're breaking our *rule. . . .*"

While at the cabin, two subjects were strictly off limits: Tony's job and my mother.

His eyebrows shrugged above the steel gray eyes. "I know, but it's been awfully quiet out there. You know, like in the old cowboy movies? *Too* quiet?"

By this he meant that Mother hadn't gotten herself (and me) tangled up in another murder of late. In other words, police business — *Tony's* business. In Mother's slight defense, sometimes she got us tangled up in the county *sheriff's* business instead. . . .

I said, "We'll start shooting the reality show in another month, and that should keep her out of mischief. Or anyway, occupied. For a change, she doesn't have murder on the mind." I lay my head back on his shoulder. "I have to admit I am *enjoy-*

ing this lull."

Which was why I wanted to stop time.

"Ditto," Tony said.

Such a way with words, my guy.

We fell into a comfortable, cozy silence.

Have you ever been at a restaurant and noticed a couple at another table hardly speaking to each other throughout their entire meal? And you thought, well, there's a marriage (relationship) in trouble. *Au contraire!* Perhaps they *prefer* silence. Take Tony and me — I was constantly being subjected to Mother's jabbering, and he had a stressful, high-pressure job, people yakking at him all day.

So we took it easy on each other.

As if contradicting that, Tony looked right at me and said, "Don't you think it's about time we talk about . . . you know — *us*?"

I squirmed.

Okay, fine — that subject wasn't Mother and it wasn't the police department, either. But the topic wasn't necessarily one I was anxious to explore. Our blossoming relationship had recently become complicated when Tony discovered he wasn't divorced.

I realize that sounds about as likely as remembering you forgot to put your clothes on before leaving the house, but let me explain.

Several years ago, when Tony Cassato was a police detective in Trenton, New Jersey, he testified against a New Jersey crime family, and his own family — that is, his wife and daughter — was forced into the Witness Protection Program. Mrs. Cassato, whom I'd never met, had been livid that Tony put them in danger, and soon served him with divorce papers, which he'd dutifully signed and returned to her lawyer.

But it turned out the papers were never officially filed. Perhaps his wife had second thoughts about ending the marriage, or wanted to maintain some kind of hold over her husband.

Whatever the reason, Tony had been unable to locate her since she and the daughter were still in WITSEC, and even after he'd left the program, Tony honored Mrs. Cassato's desire — conveyed to him by federal officers — not to be contacted by him.

"Can we talk about us later?" I demurred, explaining, "Today has been just too perfect."

Well, except for the cheesecake. The first one, I mean.

"All right, honey," he said. "But *soon,* okay?"

"I promise."

"Can't put it off forever."

"Right."

As always, first-line-of-defense Rocky heard a noise outside before we did, raising his large head off the floor to emit a long low growl, his alert eyes going to Tony.

Then I heard the snap of dry twigs and pinecones beneath car wheels, and I gave Tony a sharp look of concern, feeling his body ever so slightly stiffen.

Sushi, rousing from her slumber, emitted a high yap, better late than never from our second line of defense. Maybe third. Make that fourth. . . .

We had a right to be nervous. Last summer, Tony and I were seated on this very couch when a hired killer sent by the New Jersey mob fired bullets through the cabin windows *(Antiques Knock-Off)*. We managed to escape, and the contract on Tony's life has since been withdrawn (thanks to Mother) (but that's another story) *(Antiques Con)*.

Still, the memory of that night was all too fresh, and it had meant a long, lonely separation between us when Tony was hustled back into WITSEC.

I followed Tony to the window, where a powder blue four-door sedan was pulling up to the cabin's front porch.

The car stopped, and the front passenger

19

door opened, and Mother got out.

As I breathed a sigh of relief, Tony commented wryly, "For once I'm glad it's her."

My sigh of relief was in part because Mother hadn't driven herself. She was notoriously unlicensed, her driving privilege getting lifted more times than Joan Rivers's face (RIP).

"Thanks for the ride, Frannie!" Mother called to the driver, one of her gal pals. "Toodles!"

As the vehicle pulled away, Mother headed toward the porch with the swinging arms and determined purpose of an invading army.

Sushi and Rocky, having recognized Mother's voice, scrambled over each other to get to the front door as Mother sailed in without knocking.

Mother was statuesque and still quite attractive at her undisclosed age — porcelain complexion, straight nose, wide mouth, wavy silver hair pulled back in a loose chignon. The only downside to her appearance were the large, terribly out of style glasses that magnified her blue eyes to owl-like size.

She was decked out in a fall outfit from her favorite clothing line, Breckenridge, an orange top featuring a pumpkin patch

20

and green slacks (no pumpkin patch, thankfully). Mother was enamored of the collection because every season was color coordinated, making getting dressed a no-brainer. (She'd had me in Garanimals until I was twelve.)

After affording each dog a quick pat on the head, Vivian Borne said in a cheerful rush of words, "Hello, dear! And hello to you, too, Chiefie! Sorry to disturb your tête-à-tête, and I realize I risked catching you in flagrante, but I have simply *wonderful* news."

Tony and I had returned to the couch, with the resignation of defeated warriors, and Mother plopped down between us, squeezing in to make space.

She announced, with just a little more pomp than somebody about to break a champagne bottle over the prow of a ship, "I am sure you will be as thrilled as I was to hear that I have been asked . . . are you ready for this?"

Probably not.

She raised a hand in a grand, skywardly pointing finger gesture. "I have been asked to perform this coming weekend . . . drum roll, *please!* . . . at Old York! At the New Vic itself!"

When not involved in amateur sleuthery, or co-running our antiques shop, Mother

21

was active in community theater. In case you haven't guessed. And saying she was "active" in community theater might be an understatement. How about rabidly active?

Since my idea of wonderful news was an unexpected windfall of cash from a dead distant relative, my response was perhaps less than Mother had expected. Specifically, a tepid, "That's nice."

Tony's was a tad better: "You don't say." At least he'd gotten to where he didn't automatically give her a dirty look.

Still, these two responses took the wind out of Mother's sails, though her boat on the ocean of life never stayed still for long, and she responded with plenty of spare wind.

"Apparently," she huffed grandly, "you don't understand the importance of the offer, the opportunity, that has come my way. Let me enlighten you. Old York usually imports professional talent from the Guthrie, or New York. But on this occasion, they have chosen to book *me* for their fall fete instead."

Old York was a little town about sixty miles away that fancied itself a displaced English hamlet, hence the fall fete.

"What do you mean, fate?" Tony asked, probably thinking he wouldn't mind booking her himself. "Like cast your fate to the wind?"

"It's a kind of fair," she said, "with an English accent."

That had a nice double meaning, though it probably was just an accident, and I decided not to point out to her that *fete* was French. Mother was already miffed with us and her wit was likely on hold.

I frowned. "Isn't it a little late for the fete organizers to be asking you? I mean . . . this coming *weekend*?"

Mother shrugged. "As fate would have it — that's F-A-T-E fate, Chief Cassato — influenza struck the New York troupe who'd been hired. But this late booking provides the perfect opportunity for me to perform my version of" — she cupped her hand over her mouth and whispered — "the Scottish play."

"The what play?" Tony asked.

"Macbeth," I said.

"Dear!" Mother blurted.

I went on: "It's an old actor's superstition, not saying *'Macbeth'* in a theater. Mother takes it a step further by never saying it at all."

Her eyes went wide and her nostrils flared. "It is not just the superstition of *old* actors! Even the young ones respect it, and I would thank you, Brandy, to honor it, as well."

"Sure," I said with a shrug.

Tony asked politely, "What's your version of the, uh, Scotch play, Vivian?"

"*Scottish* play, Chief. In my rendition, I play all the parts in a sixty-minute condensation of my own creation," Mother said proudly. "Shakespeare was a good writer, but he runs to the long-winded and needs occasional editing."

"Okay."

Her eyes behind the lenses were huge. "You've heard the old expression of someone with more than one job wearing multiple hats? Well, I take that to heart, literally. I wear a different hat for each character I'm bringing to life."

To Tony's credit, he didn't flinch. Or smirk. He just said, "Interesting."

She twisted on the couch toward him. "Perhaps you would like me to reserve a seat for you in the audience? As the star, I'm sure I'll have comps for special guests."

Behind her back, I mouthed a silent but emphatic, *"No!"*

Tony's eyes went from me to Mother. "I'll try to make it, Viv. Sounds . . . unique."

And I shut my eyes. Perhaps when I opened them, I would find I'd been dreaming.

"Wonderful!" Mother chirped. "Now, I'm afraid I must spirit Brandy away from this cozy nest. She and I have a lot to do before we leave for Old York! Miles to go before we sleep. That's Robert Frost, not Shakespeare, by the way."

I gave Tony a shrug and he just smiled and nodded a little.

There was never any doubt that I would be a part of Mother's "gig." First off, due to those previously mentioned vehicular infractions, Mother couldn't drive herself anywhere. And second of all, I was in charge of the hats.

Mother stood, half bowed, and made a ridiculously grand hand gesture; it was going to be a long weekend. "I'll give you two lovebirds a moment together. Or do you need longer? I can arrange a brief nature hike for myself. Just give me a window!"

What, for her to peek in?

"No," I said, "that's all right. Just a few minutes is fine."

"Splendid!"

And she made her exit.

I scooted closer to Tony. "Thanks for not suggesting she take the path that ends in a drop-off to the river."

He paused and squinted, as if that hadn't occurred to him, and he wished it had. But he said, "You're welcome."

"You're not . . . *serious* about going to Mother's one-woman *Macbeth* show, are you?"

He slipped an arm around me. "Your mother's plays are always, uh, unusual experiences . . . and the fete sounds like fun."

I nodded. "Could be at that — especially if you stayed overnight."

I gave him a kiss to seal our fate. (Okay, I promise not to do much of that.) (Straining to use the word *fate,* I mean — I'll kiss Tony as much as I please.)

Five minutes later, I was sliding behind the wheel of our Ford C-Max, with Mother riding shotgun and Sushi settled on her lap. Then I drove down the cabin's narrow pine-tree-lined lane, the setting sun winking through the bows, finally turning onto River Road to head south toward Serenity.

A captive audience of one — Sushi having curled into a ball and gone to sleep — I listened as Mother gave me a history lesson of Old York that I didn't recall requesting.

"In the mid-eighteen hundreds," she was saying, "the village was founded by several English families who drew up a charter decreeing that their British ancestry must never be 'forsaken or forgotten.' "

26

"Still holding a grudge about that little American uprising, huh?"

She ignored that. "Which is why to this day, visiting Old York is like taking a trip across the pond to a small English hamlet."

"Only not so expensive."

"Was that my pan?"

"Where?"

"Back there! By the side of the road. It looked just like my favorite cheesecake pan!"

I said, "One cheesecake pan looks pretty much like another."

"I would *swear . . .*"

"Haven't I been saying it's time for your optical checkup?"

Since Mother had been minding our store all day, and I had cleaned up the kitchen at home, she couldn't know the pan was hers. Not for sure.

"Yes, you have, dear," Mother sighed. "But they always try to sell me new, smaller frames, and these vintage specs are exactly to *my* specs."

She meant those oversize glasses of hers that dated back decades; at least she'd stopped having the lower half tinted a pale pink, like blush.

"Mother?"

"Yes, dear?"

"This trip to Old York? If you want me to

come along and be your hat mistress, you have to promise me one thing."

"Continue."

"You'll leave your fake British accent at home."

A moment passed before she answered. "Bob's your uncle, dear."

I took my eyes off the road long enough to give her a look.

She gave me one in return — of innocence. "What? You didn't say a word about not using British expressions."

A TRASH 'N' TREASURES TIP

Use caution when buying a foreign antique that you know nothing about, because that lack of even rudimentary knowledge makes it harder to spot a reproduction or fake. But don't bother trying to convince Mother that her Ming dynasty vase is anything but priceless.

CHAPTER TWO:
ALL THAT GLISTERS
IS NOT GOLD

The following Thursday morning, with my friend Joe Lange securely behind the counter of our antiques shop during our absence, Mother and I packed the trunk of the car with everything we might need for a four-day getaway. That included casual clothes, good walking shoes, Sushi's bed and food, plus the hats and wardrobe for the play. But also, most crucially, our medications.

Yes, we were a pill-happy little group — lithium for Mother's bipolar disorder, Prozac for my depression, and insulin for Sushi's diabetes (well, a shot in her case). Old York was sixty miles away, so I didn't relish driving home and back except for an emergency.

Mother had on another Breckenridge slacks outfit (green) and I was in a crisp white blouse and, taking a breather from jeans, a khaki-colored skirt with zipper pockets, and leopard-print Sam Edelman shoes.

Around noon, we bid good-bye to Serenity so we could say hello to Great Britain, or anyway a reasonable facsimile. I was once again behind the wheel, Mother beside me, and Sushi in her foam bed in back, the Three Musketeers headed west, all for Mother, Mother for all.

To keep my stress level down, and prevent Mother from jabbering all the way, I put on a CD collection of old forties and fifties radio shows that we both enjoyed — *Bob and Ray, Fibber McGee and Molly, The Great Gildersleeve* . . . but I skipped forward at any *Aldrich Family* episodes. *"HEN-REE! HENRY ALDRICH!" "Coming, Mother . . ."*

You see, when I was little and naughty, Mother used to substitute my name (*"BRAN-DEE! BRANDY BORNE!"*). I had no idea what she was referring to until years later when we started listening to old radio shows in the car. All I knew was it was annoying.

An hour later, we took a turn off the main highway at a Monty Python–style pointing-finger sign to Old York, and in another few minutes were bumping along a narrow cobblestone street lined with hedgerows, passing by quaint stone cottages with grass-thatched roofs, many set behind arbors

30

entwined with roses.

As we entered the village proper, Mother sat forward, peering out the windshield, *ooh*ing and *ahh*ing at the English architecture. "Just look at those mullioned windows!"

What's a mullioned window? (You might well ask.) Beats me. I knew a little something about architecture, but Mother was the authority. And if you want to hear the definition of mullioned windows, and you're too lazy to check Google, you'll have to ask her yourself. Me, I'm in charge of hats.

Arriving at ground zero, the village green, I made a slow go-around the immaculate square park, where a lovely white band shell surrounded by vibrantly colorful fall mums perched like the centerpiece of a beautifully set table.

Sushi had climbed from the backseat to my lap, and now stuck her head out my open window to sniff at the recently mowed grass, her happy bark seeming to say, "Heaven! New territory!"

Eek. Had I remembered to pack the doggie baggies?

Quaint little shops rimmed the green on all four sides, on streets named Manchester, Brighton, Cambridge, and London. The styles of the buildings — Gothic, Tudor, and Queen Anne (told you I knew a little about architecture) — were as diverse as the shops themselves, each vying for attention by way of latticework, etched glass, whimsical signage, and flowers, flowers, flowers, in window boxes and hanging planters, even climbing stone walls.

The hamlet was so breathtakingly beautiful I had to pull the car over into a slanted parking space to take it all in.

Could this be paradise?

Mother was saying, "Good choice of a spot, dear. This is right in front of where we'll be staying."

I peered through the windshield for a look at our residence for the next few days: a three-story white stucco building with vertical black half-beams, a rustic sign over the entrance depicting a white horse being brushed by a groomer, with the words: THE HORSE AND GROOM INN.

Mother was already out of the car, and I joined her on the redbrick sidewalk, Sushi in hand.

"Well," she enthused, "isn't this inn just the quaintest thing!"

Perhaps a little too much so. In spite of the array of colorful flowers, the hotel seemed a little shabby on the outside, which made me worry about the inside, especially since a second sign next to the entrance —

freestanding with removable letters — read: WELCOME — ROTTEN ROOMS AND GIN. Some prankster had rearranged what must have said, WELCOME TO THE HORSE AND GROOM INN, the discarded letters littering the brick sidewalk nearby.

Mother either didn't notice this warning, or chose to ignore it, plucking Sushi from my hands. "Get the luggage, dear."

I complied, retrieving the suitcases from the trunk. Then the visiting diva held open the inn's heavy, slightly warped wooden door while I struggled in.

For a moment we stood in the entryway, our eyes adjusting from the bright sun to the dimness of the interior, which was compounded by dark wood paneling and sparse, narrow windows. A low wood-beamed ceiling added a sense of claustro-phobia, while a musty smell gave an unwel-come greeting.

To the right was a small lounging area where a few well-worn chairs were posi-tioned in front of an unlit stone fireplace. Above the mantel hung the head of a mangy moose, one antler askew, as if tipping its hat.

Hats again.

To the left was a dining area, a tad more cheerful, with red-checkered cloths on the tables, along with small floral centerpieces. The walls were covered with an assortment of colorful if faded prints of horses and hunting themes, which made the idea of lingering over a meal a little more palatable. But I could have spent the better part of an afternoon straightening those frames.

I glanced at Mother, who must have sensed my misgivings.

"We already have reservations," she whispered.

"Oh, I have reservations all right," I said.

But Mother charged ahead with Sushi to the small registration desk, prompting me with, "Bran-*dee* . . ."

"Coming, Mother," I said, falling in behind, lugging the cases.

A middle-aged man with thinning gray hair and permanent frown lines on his oblong face stood behind the counter, peering into the screen of a computer that probably dated at least to the year Mother purchased her oversize eyeglass frames.

After ignoring us for a few moments, he called over his shoulder, "*Celia!* Dearest! Guests."

A woman's shrill voice cut back through the open door of an office beyond.

"Seabert, I'm on the *phone*!" Her voice lowered, but could still be heard. "Yes, I *know* — I'd miss all of my programs if we didn't have a satellite dish hidden under those fake vines on the roof . . . and don't you dare tell any of the other trustees!"

Seabert turned toward the office. "Shall I handle it then? Wouldn't want to disturb you when you're busy."

The woman continued with her phone conversation. "When is she going in for that nip and tuck? Thursday?"

Oh my God, we were checking into *Fawlty Towers*! The sign, the moose, the rudeness . . .

Seabert turned our way with an overly forced smile. "I do apologize — my wife, Celia, usually runs reception. Now, how may I help you?"

Mother, unfazed, said sweetly, "Vivian and Brandy Borne? B-O-R-N-E. I think you'll find we have two rooms reserved."

I'd long ago stopped sharing a room with Mother after her snoring drove me into countless bathrooms to sleep in the tub. And no amount of pillows and blankets makes that a picnic.

I added, "Across the hall from each other, if possible." Even the thickest adjacent hotel-room wall was no match for Mother's nocturnal broadcasts.

The man frowned at his computer screen.

35

"Borne, you say? I'm afraid we don't have anything under that name, and we're all full this weekend, due to the fete."

Before we had a chance to respond to this unfortunate news, Celia charged out of the office.

"Seabert," she snapped, "I'll handle this." The woman waved a hand at her husband. "Do something about that antler. It's off-putting."

In her late forties or early fifties, Seabert's better half wore her dyed blond hair short, overly teased and sprayed in place. Her facial features were attractive, but made harsh by too much makeup, and her pink pastel suit was a decade out of style.

Are they doing Fawlty Towers? *I wondered. Is this a fun bit of shtick for hip guests?*

As Seabert slunk off to deal with the moose, Celia turned to us, saying pleasantly, "I *do* apologize for my husband . . . he's having a bad decade. We indeed have your reservations. Millicent Marlowe made them under her name."

Lifting a hand and her chin, Mother said, "We're in Old York for the dramatic presentation. I'm the talent, this is my staff."

If the staff had a rod, I wouldn't have used it to comfort her.

Mrs. Fawlty, that is, Celia, consulted the

computer. "Yes, two rooms. And we can put you across the hall from each other, since you are the first of our weekend guests to arrive."

"I believe our meals are to be included," Mother said regally.

With a smile so patient it lapsed into patronizing, the faux Mrs. Fawlty said, "Your meals are indeed included with your rooms, and there's grass just behind the inn for your adorable little poochie's purposes."

Our hostess turned and plucked two old-fashioned keys with wooden tags from their hooks on the wall, then handed them to Mother.

"The dining area," Celia said, "will be serving the evening meal at five o'clock, and breakfast is available from seven until eleven — lunch you'll need to catch on your own." She paused for a breath. "If there's anything I can do to make your stay more pleasant, please don't hesitate to contact me. We're Celia and Seabert, the Falwells."

Close, I thought.

I asked, "Could you point us to the New Vic Theater? I didn't spot it when we drove around the village green." I knew Mother would be wanting to go there next.

"It's just off the green, one block west," she replied. "Stratford-on-Avon Street."

Naturally.

"Anything else?" Celia smiled.

"And your lift?" Mother asked.

"Pardon? Did you need a lift somewhere?"

"She means elevator," I said.

Mother looked miffed that the faux Mrs. Fawlty didn't understand the English vernacular.

"Sadly we haven't one," she replied, then sighed deeply. "Seabert and I wanted to install an elevator, but the other trustees wouldn't sanction it."

I asked, "Other trustees?"

"Yes. I'm on the board, but there's a fuddy-duddy contingent who are against any progress."

Mother winked. "But you still managed to slip a satellite dish past 'em."

"Ah, you overheard. *That* proved easier to hide than an elevator. It wasn't until the sixties that lodging with television was even allowed — we're supposed to have indoor antennas. Can't have a thatched roof with an aerial, after all — wouldn't do!" She paused, buried her bitterness beneath a smile. "But we *were* able to finally install individual bathrooms in the rooms."

Startled, I asked, "When was that?"

"Last year. Can I get Seabert to help with the luggage?"

"No, I can manage," I replied, preferring to carry the cases up rather than bother Basil. That is, Seabert.

The stairs were next to the dining room, and I followed Mother and Sushi up, grateful our accommodations were on the second floor, not the third.

Mother took the room with a view of the village green, while I was content to have the one facing the back parking lot, which should be quieter.

Otherwise, our rooms were identical — cramped (due to the added bathroom, only slightly larger than one in a third-class cruise ship compartment), bed with wrought-iron frame, small armoire, and a desk with chair. But the carpet looked recent, the floral wallpaper wasn't overly busy, and crisp white lace curtains hung on the single (apparently mullioned) window.

We took five minutes to settle in and unpack a few things, Sushi trotting back and forth between our two quarters, most likely trying to make up her mind where she wanted to sleep (she was immune to Mother's snoring — dogs can sleep through anything except the rustle of a potato chip bag).

Then we were off to the New Vic, taking the car rather than walking as Mother wanted to unload her/our prop hats for the show, which she'd been told was scheduled for Saturday night.

The New Vic might have been better called the New Old Vic, because it was yet another ancient building, looking decidedly oversized among its quaint residential neighbors.

We parked in a side lot, leaving Mother's gear in the trunk for the moment, then walked around to the front. I had been to the Old Vic in London early in my marriage to Roger (we'd seen Kevin Spacey perform in *Richard II* — wow!), and this old-looking New Vic was a smaller version of that theater. The building was brick Georgian architecture (like our Colonial) with a wide front overhang supported by columns, and a top triangular facade, where the comedy/tragedy masks substituted for the Old Vic's royal crest.

We went in through the middle of three wood and glass double doors, and there the New Vic's similarity to the original ceased.

A marbled foyer with a small glassed-in ticket station was to the left, a concession counter to the right. Ahead were doors to the auditorium, curving staircases on either side leading up to the balcony. With the exception of one large ceiling fixture, a relatively recent addition, the only other lighting source was a few wall sconces.

Mother, whispering as if in church, said, "I wonder where we can find Millicent Marlowe?"

"Here I am, Mrs. Borne," said a woman's thin voice, so close it startled us.

The owner of the voice — and the theater — had come up behind Mother, whose stature had hidden her. She was a tiny thing, rather frail looking, knocking on eighty's door at least, with white hair cut short in a curly perm. She wore a red sweater, navy slacks, and the kind of sensible shoes Mother puts on when her bunions are particularly bothersome.

The woman extended a bony hand to Mother. "Please," she said, "call me Millie . . . all my friends do."

Mother shook Millie's hand a little too gregariously and a bone or two made tiny cracks.

"My dear," Mother gushed, "what a *divine* theater you have here."

I was holding off on my opinion until after seeing the stage.

"Yes," Millie bubbled, "you may have noticed that it's a replica of the Old Victoria."

Told you.

She went on. "A bit smaller, of course. There have even been rumors of ancient tunnels, but that's probably an old wives' tale."

"Merry ones, no doubt!" Mother said. "From Windsor!"

"No doubt!" Our hostess's eyes, which had been flitting nervously, settled on me like friendly insects. "And you must be Brandy."

I didn't shake her hand, mine being full of Sushi. "Pleased to meet you," I said with a smile and a nod, adding, "I'll be assisting Mother."

"My daughter," Mother said grandly, "is in charge of wardrobe and props."

The wardrobe *was* props, but never mind.

"How delightful!" Millie said, clasping her hands. "A family affair. I can't believe you've never visited us before, Vivian!"

"Oh, well, it's always been something I meant to do. So many conflicts with my own acting schedule."

I knew darn well why we'd never been here before — Vivian Borne wasn't going to support an area theater that didn't involve her.

Millie was saying, "I do appreciate you coming at such late notice, as do the trustees who put on the fete. They will be receiving

42

the proceeds — after your payment, of course — the money going to help better the town."

"How nice," Mother said perfunctorily.

"Yes. I have a contract in the office for you to sign, but we can do that later. Right now I'd like to show you around. Unfortunately, you'll only have a few days to rehearse."

"Not to worry," Mother chortled. "I'm an old pro."

That was the only context in which you will ever hear Mother refer to herself as an "old" anything. I preferred to think of her as a well-aged ham.

"Oh, I know you are a *wonderful,* creative actor," Millie said to Mother. "I saw you perform once, at the Iowa State Fair."

Mother's eyes got larger than even those lenses could handle. "You did? Why, I wish you had come backstage and spoken to me afterward!"

"Well, there *was* no backstage, really. And there was quite a crowd."

Mother beamed. "Ah yes, I recall. I pulled quite an audience that afternoon."

I was frowning. "When did you perform at the Iowa State Fair?"

"When you were living in Chicago, dear. Now, then, Millie —"

43

"Now wait," I said. "What play were you in?"

"It wasn't exactly a play, child. A play is only one kind of theatrical exhibition."

"Well, what was *this* one?"

Her hand fluttered like a butterfly. "I read poems submitted by school children. They had a shared subject."

Millie was nodding, smiling admiringly. "Oh, yes. 'Ode to a Butter Cow.' "

"Now," Mother said, "about my dressing room —"

"You mean," I said, "you gave dramatic readings by schoolchildren standing next to the cow carved from butter?"

"That's one way to put it," Mother sniffed.

That was the only way to put it.

Millie was radiant. "It was a transcendent performance. You'd have been *proud* of your mother."

My mouth was dry, but I couldn't transcend it, so I asked, "Is there a vending machine around?"

Millie pointed a slightly twisted finger toward the box office area. "You'll find several down that hallway, dear."

I nodded. "You two go ahead with the tour — I'll catch up."

Mother looped arms with the woman, as if they had been friends forever, and as they

44

moved toward the auditorium doors, I went in search of caffeine, figuring our afternoon here might stretch into early evening, Mother most likely wanting to do a run-through. When you're in charge of hats, you have to stay on top of things.

I had just gotten a strong-tasting coffee when a young man in his twenties exited the box office. His shoulder-length hair was as black as the rest of his outfit — T-shirt, jeans, high-top tennies — but his complexion was so white it was startling, especially the skin around his multiple tattoos. His face was angular, nose thin and long, mouth wide, and each earlobe had been stretched with a circular earring making a hole you could see through.

"I'm Chad," he said blandly, "Millicent's grandson and the New Vic's artistic director." He showed no particular interest in me, his grandmother, or the position he'd just mentioned, for that matter.

"I'm Brandy Borne — Vivian's daughter and assistant."

Sushi, transferred to one hand while I held the coffee with the other, took an immediate dislike to Chad by way of a low growl.

Filling an awkward pause, I said, "Mother is grateful for the booking."

He shrugged again. "We had no choice."

I nodded. "Because that New York company cancelled."

He closed his eyes and opened them again, bored with me, and life. "There *wasn't* any New York company."

I frowned. "I don't understand. . . ."

He sighed, burdened as he was with having the weight of the world — or this theater, anyway — on his shoulders. "You *will* understand, Ms. Borne, after you have a look around. Everything is so outdated and antiquated that I can't get anyone of any importance at all to appear here."

I didn't appreciate the obvious insult to my mother. Like all children, only I have the right to make snide remarks about my parents.

So there was a little edge when I said, "So update the theater. Or is it a matter of money?"

His laugh could not have sounded more hollow if he'd done it down a well. "Money in part. Grandmother once had quite a pile, but over the years it got sunk into this monstrosity. Not that it did much good."

"No?"

He shrugged. "We've been running in place for years. Strictly Shakespeare. Other theaters in tourist-trap towns do musicals and murder mysteries and other crowd-pleasing stuff. But Grandmother is on the board of —"

"Don't tell me — the good ol' board of trustees. Keepers of the status quo, circa a couple hundred years ago." I tilted my head. "How many of these darling people are there?"

"Six."

"And they're steadfastly against change?"

"Three of them are. And that makes for a stalemate on every subject, meaning nothing gets done."

What made me think of Washington, DC, all of a sudden?

I asked, "Where does your grandmother stand?"

"She thinks the New Vic is just fine as it is, even if attendance *has* fallen off terribly."

"I can understand your frustration," I said, rolling my eyes.

He narrowed his. "It was Grandmother who booked your mother — something about a one-woman show? And I assume it has something to do with Shakespeare."

"Yes to both," I said, but offered no more details, not wanting Mother to be tossed out by the artistic director on her artistic rear before curtain time.

He nodded. "Well, it's *something* anyway. Got to have some damn thing onstage for

47

this weekend."

Such enthusiasm.

Realizing at last that he might have been just a touch rude, he said, "I'm sure it will be fine."

"Well, I promise it'll be memorable," I said with a smile. Especially if I mixed up the hats.

Mother was rushing along the corridor toward us.

"Young man!" she said, flushed and out of breath. "Young man, would there happen to be a hospital here in Old York?"

Alarmed, I said, "Mother, aren't you well?"

"Tickety boo, dear." Her eyes returned to Chad. "*Have* you a hospital?"

"No, no . . . but there's one in the next town over."

Mother put hands on hips. "All right. Well, what do you use in the village for a morgue? Perhaps there's a funeral home."

Chad, frowning, asked what I was thinking: "What in the world do you need a morgue for?"

Mother flapped her arms like a goose before takeoff. "Not me, my good man . . . *Millie!* She seemed to be taking an onstage bow and then just went all the way down. I do believe she's dropped dead."

A Trash 'n' Treasures Tip

Before purchasing an antique in a foreign country, research similar items from several different sources to determine a realistic price. Then don't forget to haggle. Mother knows how to ask, "Is that your best price?" in Danish, Swedish, German, French, Spanish, and Japanese. (If she knew Chinese, that Ming dynasty vase might not be a sore spot.)

CHAPTER THREE: DEATH IS A FEARFUL THING

After Mother made the pronouncement to Chad and me that Millicent Marlowe had taken her final encore, the three of us hurried into the auditorium.

This was my first time inside the rather small theater, and my immediate impression was one of gloom. Mother always referred to any theater as "she," much the way a captain speaks of his ship. Well, this lady really needed a makeover, including a new wardrobe. A little perfume to cover the musty smell wouldn't hurt, either.

As I headed down the center aisle with its red, threadbare carpet, I could see Millie's slumped form up on the stage, on her back.

A man knelt over her, holding one of her limp hands, almost as if he were proposing. Perhaps forty, he wore a denim work shirt and paint-splattered jeans, his average features distinguished by a pair of aviator-style glasses and a receding hairline.

Chad leapt up onto the apron of the stage in an almost theatrical flourish, which Mother and I did not imitate, taking the more sensible route of the short flight of stairs on the left.

The kneeling man looked up at Chad. "I'm . . . I'm afraid she's gone."

"What on earth happened, Fred?" Chad asked, a slight tremble in his voice. "Were you here with her?"

Fred released Millie's hand, stood, gestured to Mother, as she and I approached. "Your grandmother was introducing me to Mrs. Borne when she suddenly just . . . went down." The man shook his head sadly. "It really was almost like a bow or a curtsy."

Mother whispered to me, "That's Fred Hackney. He constructs the sets and runs things backstage."

I nodded, then whispered back: "That's Chad Marlowe, the grandson. Artistic director."

Digging out his cell phone, Chad was saying, "I'll call for the paramedics."

Mother asked, "Do you have local paramedics, Mr. Marlowe?"

He shook his head. "Next town over, fifteen miles away."

"Then that would be a waste of resources."

51

"What?"

Rather bluntly, Mother said, "Who you *should* call, young man, is the county sheriff."

"The sheriff?" Chad asked, frowning. "Lady, my grandmother was eighty-two. She had a bad heart. Took medicine for it. Obviously she had a heart attack."

Mother arched an eyebrow. "Did she, dear?"

His frown deepening, Chad took a few steps toward her. "What are you implying?"

"I'm not implying a single solitary thing, young man," Mother answered. "But I have my reasons why I think someone with authority should be called here to . . . oversee . . . the aftermath of this tragedy."

And that someone would be Mother's friendly adversary, Sheriff Rudder, since this was Serenity County and Old York was under his jurisdiction.

Chad snapped, "Well I think *that's* a waste of resources — isn't he in Serenity? That's sixty miles from here!"

But Mother had turned away from him, walking downstage to make the call on her cell — she had the sheriff on speed-dial.

Chad gaped at me. His long dark hair and angular face seemed appropriately theatrical as he gestured to the dead woman. "So my grandmother is . . . *what?* . . . just going to be left flung on the floor like a sandbag until the sheriff drives all the way here?"

I said gently, "If my mother has reasons why Sheriff Rudder should come, I can assure you they're valid."

Usually. Sometimes. Probably. Maybe.

Fred, who'd remained mute through this exchange, touched Chad's arm. "I can get her a blanket — there's one in the dressing room."

Millie's grandson sighed, then nodded.

Fred exited stage left while Mother rejoined Chad and me, having completed her call.

"We're in luck!" she said, inappropriately cheerful. "Sheriff Rudder is a mere twenty minutes away, working on something or other that's undoubtedly less important than this. And if I know that man, and I do, he'll be here sooner than later, because my calls are something he *always* takes seriously."

There had been a time when the sheriff routinely ignored Mother's calls, but — thanks to her relentless persistence — Rudder had come to realize it was better to deal with them right now, and get it over with.

Fred returned with the blanket. He began to spread it over Millie, then stopped, eyes going to Mother. The man sensed, correctly, that she was in charge.

"I see no reason for her not to be comfortable," she said, nodding approval.

Chad's back had been to this, but now he whirled to her. *"Comfortable?"* he mocked. "Maybe Grandmother would like a *pillow?"*

Shaking his head, he walked to the apron, jumped down, then took a front row seat, slumping there, arms crossed, his face long with sorrow and disgust.

Mother dispatched me to go wait outside to meet Rudder, and I did so, taking Sushi with me. I put her down on a little patch of grass and she blissfully took advantage of new territory, wholly unaware of the tragic circumstances. Sometimes it *is* a dog's life.

According to my Chico's watch, I had been waiting outside the theater doors for twelve minutes when Rudder's light blue car with its Serenity County Sheriff's door insignias pulled up. He was behind the wheel and alone; he got out and strode toward me with that sideways John Wayne walk of his. Maybe, like Mother, he had bunions.

Whatever the case, in that tan uniform, the sheriff made a tall, commanding figure, graying just a little at the temples. The walk wasn't the only thing that made Mother wistfully comment, from time to time, that Rudder reminded her of the middle-aged Duke.

The sheriff planted himself in front of me like a big oak tree. "What's this about a murder that your mother's going on about?"

"Call it a suspicious death." I wasn't ready to commit to the *m* word yet. "Millicent Marlowe collapsed, while showing mother around. Miss Marlowe owns, or owned, this theater."

Rudder frowned in recollection. "I believe I know her, or anyway met her — older woman? Why weren't the paramedics called?"

"Mother wanted you to see her first."

He sighed. "She does have her own way of doing things. Damnit, this better not be a waste of time — I'm shorthanded as it is. Where is she?"

"Mother?"

"The dead woman."

"On the stage."

"And your mother?"

"On the stage."

Rudder winced.

Just before we moved inside, he asked, "What are you and Vivian doing here, anyway? Aren't you two a little ways off your beat?"

Briefly, I filled him in.

With Sushi in my arms, I had to hustle to keep up with the lawman's long stride as he crossed the lobby. Entering the auditorium, Rudder was met by an agitated Chad, who'd come rushing up the center aisle.

"Sheriff," he said, as if making a point in an already long under-way argument, "my grandmother died from a heart attack, and that's *all* there is to it!"

Rudder held up a traffic-cop palm. "Let's back it up, son, and start with your name."

"Chad Marlowe. Artistic director of the theater. As I said, Millicent is, *was,* my grandmother."

The sheriff's eyes traveled past Chad to the stage, and the small form covered by the blanket. "Sorry for your loss. Please take a seat down front, Mr. Marlowe."

Rudder stepped around Chad and proceeded toward the stage. I followed with Sushi.

From the stage, Mother called, "*Sheriff Rudder!* I'm so very pleased to see you. We're so fortunate you were in the neighborhood."

This greeting was met with stony silence as the sheriff ascended the steps and went to the body, then squatted in front of it to slowly pull back the blanket. He checked the woman's throat for a pulse.

After a moment, he looked up at Mother. "Well, Vivian, you're correct that this woman is deceased . . . but what was the idea of calling me to the scene?"

"Isn't it obvious? Look at her arms, Sheriff."

Taking Millie's nearest arm, Rudder noted the pushed-up sleeve of the red sweater, revealing a large purple area.

Rudder sighed, then stood. "Hematoma."

Chad, in the front row, asked, "What did you say?"

Before the sheriff could reply, Mother did, calling out helpfully, "Hematoma, dear! Symptom of an overdose of blood thinner medication."

Fred, who had been standing motionless near the stage-left wing, chimed in: "Dang it, anyway. Millie probably lost track of how much medication she took."

Rudder's head swiveled, as if noticing the man for the first time, though I knew very well that the sheriff had taken everything in already. "And you would be?"

"Fred Hackney. Carpenter, general handyman around here. I make the sets and props."

Rudder approached him. "And your opinion that the woman overdosed herself —

that's based on what exactly?"

Fred began studying his feet to avoid Rudder's stare.

"Well, sir, I've noticed that Millie hasn't been as . . . you know, *sharp* lately. Guess she was gettin' on at that."

Chad stood at his seat and called up: "Grandmother *has* been awfully forgetful lately."

Rudder moved to the edge of the stage and stared down at the young man. "You know what heart medication she'd been taking?"

Chad shrugged. "I'm not sure. It's not something we ever discussed. But they're these little pink pills she keeps in her purse." He gestured behind him. "Her purse in the office — do you want me to . . . ?"

"No, I'll collect it later. Stay put, if you would. Thank you."

Chad nodded, shrugged. "Okay. But I did see her take one of those pills, just this morning."

"What time?"

"Ah . . . around ten, I think."

Rudder's eyes narrowed. "Have you notified any other family members yet about your grandmother?"

Chad shook his head. "No one to notify. I'm her only living relative."

I found that of interest; Mother did, too, judging by her slightly raised eyebrows.

Rudder turned toward Mother. "You and Brandy can go."

"What's that?" Mother's expression was that of a woman who'd had water splashed in her face.

"I said," he spoke tightly, "you both can go. Thank you for the call, Vivian. That will be all."

Mother planted her feet. "Are you quite sure, Sheriff Rudder? Because, let me tell you —"

"Let me tell *you,* Vivian. Leave."

Now she put her fists on her hips, Superman style. "Can you at least assure me that there *will* be an autopsy?"

The sheriff's endless arm stretched out as he pointed toward the rear of the theater, in a don't-darken-my-door-again manner.

She sighed, her body relaxing into defeat. "Very well. We're at the Horse and Groom Inn if you need us."

Which garnered only a grunt.

Banished, Mother and I, with Sushi still in my arms, made our exit down the steps, up the center aisle, through the lobby and toward the front doors. That was when Mother made a sudden detour down the hallway where the vending machines lined a wall like suspects in a police lineup.

I figured she'd worked up a thirst telling the sheriff how to do his job, but then Mother veered into the office that was just before the vending machines and behind the box office.

Catching up to her, I whispered, "What are you *doing*? The sheriff has taken over, and this isn't even vaguely our business."

"Of course it's our business, dear."

The office was a glorified cubbyhole with a single metal desk with swivel chair, a few filing cabinets, a couple of metal chairs, and plaster walls hung with framed posters of past New Vic productions.

Mother had found Millie's purse on the cluttered desktop and was opening it.

"Dear," Mother said, "if you don't want to be a party to what I'm about to do, you should leave."

I stayed.

You may question my sanity — I certainly do, often enough — but allowing Mother to conduct a criminal investigation unsupervised is like opening the cabinets under the kitchen sink and setting down your two-year-old with a jaunty, "Have fun!"

Using a tissue from her pocket, Mother pulled out the prescription bottle, studied the information label for a moment, then

60

removed the cap. She poured the round pink pills into a palm, counted them, then returned the pills to the bottle and the bottle to the purse, and the purse to where she'd found it on the desk.

Then we skedaddled.

"Well?" I asked, once we were in our car in the side lot. I was leaning on the wheel and I had not turned the key.

"The medication Millie was taking is indeed a blood thinner," Mother said, "generally given to someone who has suffered a heart attack."

"So Millie may have died from *another* heart attack."

"I doubt that very much, dear."

"Because of the hema thing, you mean."

"That's certainly a factor. But a more important one is the date of the prescription, and the number of pills left in the bottle."

Like an actress gone up on her lines, Mother loved prompting. "Yes? Because?"

Giving me a self-satisfied smile, she said, "The prescription for thirty pills was filled on September the fifteenth. Millie was to take one each morning. Today is October the first. Yet there were only ten pills left."

"That's math, Mother. Don't make me do math."

"Go on, dear. It's not that difficult."

"Well . . . there should have been at least fifteen pills left in that bottle, right?"

Mother nodded sagely.

"So," I said, "Millie must have been double-dosing on more than one occasion. Out of forgetfulness, perhaps."

Mother stroked Sushi on her lap. "Or so someone wanted it to appear. It's all too easy to trot out how absentminded or even pre-Alzheimer's an older person can be."

We had arrived at our local home-away-from-home, where I found a spot in front. We got out and I noticed the outside sign had been restored to WELCOME TO THE HORSE AND GROOM INN.

Inside, Celia, in her outdated pastel pink suit, was behind the check-in counter. With a practiced smile, she asked, "And how did the Bornes like the New Vic?"

"Really a charming venue," Mother replied. "On the other hand, Millicent Marlowe is dead."

Standing behind Mother, I tried pinching her through her Spanx, with no luck. While she could be tactless, particularly on the subject of death — she was fatalistic to a fault — I was well aware that she would now be viewing every resident of Old York as a suspect.

Celia stared, agape. "Did I hear you correctly, Mrs. Borne?"

I stepped around Mother. "I'm afraid Millie suffered a fatal heart attack. One moment she was smiling, the next . . . well, I'm afraid she's gone."

"Oh, that's just terrible," Celia said, one hand to her chest. "Such a terrible loss to our community."

I nodded sympathetically. Mother was studying the woman rather coldly, looking for reactions.

Celia said, with a shrug that indicated she had a streak of fatalism, too, "Well, I can't say I'm surprised, really. She had a heart attack before. Will you excuse me?"

The innkeeper turned abruptly and disappeared into her office, where in New (not Old) York fashion she could start spreadin' the news.

Mother eyed me with a smile I can only describe as devilish. "Quite a cold reaction, don't you think?"

From the office came a faint but distinct: "Yes, a *heart* attack! . . . Yes, yes . . . I *know.* . . ."

I set Sushi down and turned to face Mother. Sushi looked up at her, too. "Vivian Borne, what is *wrong* with you?"

Since no one else was around, I thought

this was as good a time as any to get into it with her.

Mother's eyebrows went up and over her glasses and her expression was one of angelic innocence. "Why, whatever do you mean, dear?"

"You call *her* cold? How about how insensitively you're behaving? The blunt way you told Chad about Millie, and now Mrs. Falwell!"

Her chin came up. "I was merely stating the truth. Anyway, darling, you know I'm fishing for suspicious reactions."

"Can't you go fishing without such tactless bait on your line? Try a little compassion on your hook, why don't you?"

She cocked her head, like Sushi trying to understand a new word. "Dear . . . don't take this wrong . . . but have you been taking your Prozac as prescribed?"

"How about you? Taking your lithium? As prescribed?"

About once a month we were reduced to this.

Mother lowered her voice. "Dear, I have a wealth of compassion in this situation."

"Do you?"

"Yes. And it all goes to my good friend Millie."

"Your good friend Millie? You *just* met her."

"We were fellow thespians. Sisters of the stage. You should be used to my methods by now. The reactions I'm gathering will help us catch her killer."

"*If* she was killed," I reminded her. "We don't know that for sure."

"*Yet.*"

Sushi, having enough of this, barked.

I sighed. "Baby wants her supper."

Mother bestowed a smile upon me. "Then why don't we table this matter, dear, until our evening meal?"

I agreed. We knew we needed a breather from each other, and returned to our respective rooms.

An hour later, Mother and I were seated in the dining room at a table for two beneath a framed print of ferocious hounds chasing a frightened fox, the picture's once vibrant colors having faded from sunlight.

A few other customers were dining, as well — a portly couple in the dessert phase (bread pudding), and an elderly man reading a *Des Moines Register* over coffee.

Seabert, wearing a too-tight three-piece suit even more out of style than his wife's attire, came over with a wine list, which we declined.

Unhappy with our decision, he snatched up our wineglasses so they wouldn't get sullied.

"We've got shepherd's pie or bangers and mash," our host declared with an offhand finality that said there were no other options. He really was John Cleese without the comic timing.

Mother had the pie; I took the bangers.

After Seabert left — and rather than reopen the wound of her insensitivity — I shared with Mother the conversation I'd had with Chad in the vending machine hallway, just before she'd arrived with the dire news about Millie.

Mother's magnified eyes behind the large glasses narrowed to near normal size. "So the young man was opposed to how his grandmother was running the New Vic."

"Yes, and he was *especially* opposed to the way she was using her own money to keep it afloat."

Mother nodded. "The poor boy had to just sit there and watch his inheritance fritter-flutter away. I would call that a good murder motive."

I leaned across and whispered, "*Must* you see mayhem everywhere you look?"

Mother's eyebrows crawled above the rims of her glasses like caterpillars chasing a leaf.

"The way you talk, one would think I *enjoy* solving murders."

Since I wasn't at that moment drinking from my water glass, I denied the few other diners that age-old theatrical fave, the spit-take. Mother, across the table from me, was spared that refreshing spray, as well.

She put a splayed hand to her chest. "Dear, it distresses me that you think so poorly of me. Surely you must know that beneath my hard, cold mask, I am suffering from the tragedy that befell poor Millicent. . . . Oh, goodie, here comes our food!" She leaned in with a conspiratorial smile and said, "I hope the pie is as good as *my* recipe, although frankly I can't *imagine* it could be."

MOTHER'S SHEPHERD PIE
1 tbl. olive oil
1 clove garlic, crushed
1 onion, chopped
1 carrot, chopped
1 can cut green beans
1 lb. lamb, minced
1 beef cube stock
1 lb. tomatoes, chopped
3 tbl. tomato puree
1 tbl. corn flour
2 lb. potatoes

1/4 lb. butter (1 stick)
pinch of salt and pepper

Heat olive oil in a skillet, add the onion, garlic, and carrot and cook until soft. Add minced lamb and stock cube, then cook until brown and crumbly. Stir in the canned green beans, tomatoes, and tomato puree, then add the corn flour. Let simmer, stirring occasionally, for about fifteen minutes or until thickened. Meanwhile, peel and chop the potatoes and boil until soft, then mash with the butter, add salt and pepper to taste. Put the meat filling into a deep oven dish, top with the mashed potatoes, and put under broiler until the top is brown and crisp.

Mother had once made this recipe for little Brandy who refused to eat it because of the lamb. (PBS had been showing the old *Shari Lewis Show,* with the talented ventriloquist and her cute puppet, Lamb Chop.) Hamburger can be substituted for the lamb, as Mother did for me from that point on, but then what you're eating is Cottage Pie.

We were finishing our hearty meals — no complaints from either of us — when Celia swooshed over. Our hostess's big smile said she was bearing up well under the news of

Millie's death.

"I'm going to be gone for about an hour," she told us, a hand on the back of my chair. "Should you need anything, Seabert will tend to it. Ask him twice if necessary."

Mother said innocently, "I would imagine you're off to a meeting of the trustees."

Celia's smile faded. "Why . . . yes. How in heaven's name could you guess, much less know, that?"

Mother dabbed her mouth daintily with the napkin. "It just stands to reason, after Millie's sudden death."

Good lord! Was Mother actually going to come right out and say that the votes for incorporation, and bringing progress to Old York, now swung three for and two against?

But instead Mother said, "I wonder if the board might not like to have someone present a brief eulogy before my performance Saturday night?"

"Ah . . . that does sound appropriate," Celia said, somewhat blindsided. "That is, *if* there's a play at all."

Mother was quick to rise from her chair, a testament to the high quality of her double hip replacement.

Chin high, swathed in indignation, she said, "Madam! If that is *indeed* an issue, shouldn't *I* be included in this meeting? And

69

my daughter, as well, the other half of the Borne troupe. After all, we've come quite a distance."

Sixty miles.

"And might I point out," Mother added imperiously, "we gave up another engagement to take this one!"

Not really.

Celia, frowning, shaking her head, the friendly hand off the back of my chair now, said, "I'm sorry, Mrs. Borne — only trustees are allowed at our meetings."

"I see," Mother replied. "Then I guess they wouldn't be interested in hearing Millicent Marlowe's last words."

Celia's eyes widened. "Well, *I* am. What were they?"

Yes, what? Mother hadn't mentioned anything about this to me.

"I'm so sorry, Mrs. Falwell," Mother said sweetly. "I'm afraid Millie's final thoughts were intended for *all* of the trustees to hear."

Our hostess stood frowning in thought. Then, with obvious reluctance, she said, "All right — you may attend."

"My daughter, too."

"Yes, yes, yes." She checked her wristwatch. "Come to the Community Center in ten minutes — it's just across the village green, on Brighton. I'll go on ahead and

70

inform the others that you'll be dropping by."

She hurried off.

After signing the meals to our rooms, Mother and I stepped out into a brisk autumn night air that made me wish I'd brought along a jacket. The sky was nearly cloudless and the moon was full and glowing. Speaking of the moon, our unknown prankster had struck the standing sign again: WELCOME — DARN HORSE ON THE MOON.

As Mother and I cut across the lush, ivory-washed grass, I asked, "What *were* Millie's final words?"

She gave me a sideways glance. "I've been mulling that. Haven't settled on anything just yet. What do *you* think they should be?"

I stopped short, but she kept on going.

"Mother, you didn't. . . ."

"Actually, Millie didn't."

"Oh, Mother."

As I caught back up with her, she shrugged and impishly grinned. "Got us into the meeting, didn't it?"

The Community Center was on the first floor of a Tudor-style building sandwiched between a tearoom and an apothecary. After entering through an etched-glass door into a long, narrow room with a low ceiling crisscrossed by wooden beams, we moved through a sitting area where several mismatched couches and overstuffed chairs huddled around a scarred coffee table. Beyond this was an area used for meetings with banquet-style tables, both rectangular and round, set with metal folding chairs, off of which a kitchenette was home to an old refrigerator that hummed and a coffeemaker that gurgled.

Mother and I approached a round table where what I assumed to be the remaining five trustees were seated.

Celia stood, her expression pleasant. "Everyone . . . this is Vivian Borne and her daughter, Brandy. As you know, these girls were supposed to put on a play at the New Vic Saturday night."

At the words "supposed to," Mother flinched, but held her tongue. I did the same on the word "girls."

The innkeeper introduced the trustees, gesturing to each one as she went clockwise around the table.

"This is Digby Lancaster, Old York's resident land developer."

Around sixty, heavyset, Lancaster had bulldog features and a belly that strained the middle of his blue button-down shirt.

"And this is Father Cumberbatch, priest

72

at the Episcopalian Church."

Perhaps thirty-five, Cumberbatch was slender, his sandy hair unruly, his eyes a light blue. He wore the traditional dark suit with white collar.

"This is Barclay Starkadder, manager of the local museum, a favorite tourist stop of ours."

Pushing sixty, distinguished-looking in a three-piece suit, Starkadder sported carefully groomed silver hair and a neatly trimmed beard; he had the general appearance of a matinee idol gone long in the tooth.

"And, finally," Celia said, "this is Flora Payton. She owns our floral shop."

I wondered if somebody named Fawna ran the local pet shop.

Flora, about forty, was a beauty with flowing red hair, green eyes, slightly freckled translucent skin, and lips stained a startling red. She wore a fuzzy black sweater with a low neckline better suited for clubbing.

Celia sat down. No chairs were offered us.

Mother said in her faux English accent, "I'm most honored to meet you all, gentle people," and I gave her a little kick below the table line. That would be enough of that.

Only then she gave the trustees an obsequious bow — with hand gesture! *Salami,*

salami, baloney.

Their expressions ranged from bemused to appreciative.

Me? I wanted to crawl under that table and maybe suck my thumb.

Mother went on, minus the faux Britishness. "I understand there may be some hesitance among you in proceeding with the performance Saturday night . . . but I am here to share with you Millie's last words to me . . . her final words to anyone, on this mortal coil."

Everyone sat forward. Well, me, I just stood there, arms folded. This would be good. Which is to say, would be bad.

"As I held her in my arms, the lovely lady looked up at me, and somehow she summoned a smile . . . and she said . . ." Mother's voice turned raspy and she gasped for breath. "The . . . show . . . must . . . go . . . *on!*"

Roll your eyes if you must, but as for the eyes of the trustees, a few tears flowed in response and even a chin or two quivered. Shameless.

"That is *so* Millie," Celia said, sniffling, and then blew her nose into a tissue. Kind of a honk. How do people do that?

Flora, dabbing under her eyes with a lacy hanky, said, "Millicent was so dedicated to

74

that theater — keeping it afloat all these years, lately out of her own pocket. We simply *must* honor her wishes."

Barclay didn't seem so sure. "We could be perceived as being unfeeling — more interested in the box-office proceeds than being respectful of Millie."

"*What* proceeds?" Digby snorted. "That event has always lost money — broken even at best."

Mother cleared her throat. "Excuse me, but, ladies and gentlemen? I *do* have a contract with the New Vic . . ."

Which she hadn't gotten around to signing.

". . . that would have to be honored whether I perform or not. So you might as well have me perform, and take the opportunity to honor Millie with a precurtain eulogy."

The trustees exchanged looks. Then spokeswoman Celia said, "Good points, Mrs. Borne."

Father Cumberbatch, who'd been quietly listening, now spoke. "I would be happy to give a short benediction honoring Millie before the play begins. That is, if anyone is concerned about appearances or propriety."

"Bless you, Father," Mother said.

"A splendid suggestion," Barclay said.

75

Nods all around.

Celia asked, "Shall we vote on proceeding with the play?"

It was unanimous; the show would go on.

Just as Millie had asked . . .

Mother clapped her hands like a birthday girl being given a pony. "I promise you to deliver the most unforgettable performance of my theatrical life!"

A tall order, if this one really did beat her tumbling into the orchestra pit during a musical version of *Everybody Loves Opal* and getting her foot stuck in the tuba.

The door to the Community Center opened, and a slender figure blew in — Chad Marlowe. He had exchanged his black T-shirt and jeans for a suit — also black. Tie, too.

He strode right up to the table of trustees.

"Why wasn't I informed of this meeting?" he demanded. "As my grandmother's only living relative, I am entitled to take her place on the board."

The trustees exchanged wary glances.

Finally Celia spoke. "Chad, we did not wish to intrude at this sad moment. But we would like to offer our sincere sympathy in the death of —"

"Skip it," he snapped. "Why wasn't I *notified*?"

76

"Dear boy," Barclay intoned pompously, "as Celia has indicated, we did not want to bother you at this difficult time. Besides —"

"Oh, I'm *sure* that's it," Chad replied caustically.

"I was *going* to say," Barclay went on huffily, "that your appointment to the board isn't official until our next regular meeting, which is on Wednesday, at which time you will be duly installed and granted all of the rights and privileges of *any* trustee. *That* is our procedure."

"Oh . . ." The young man shifted awkwardly from one foot to the other. "Then . . . you'll be contacting me about the time of the meeting and what to expect?"

"Certainly," said Celia.

No one offered anything more.

Chad turned to leave, then swung back. "One other thing. You might like to know my position on incorporating the town." He paused for effect. "It may surprise you, since all of you know I'm personally in favor of a better future for York. But just the same, I plan on honoring my grandmother's position *against* incorporation." He smiled, and what lay behind it was unclear. "Why? Because I know she would have wanted me to."

After hearing Chad grouse about the lack of innovation at the theater, for which he very much blamed his grandmother, I found his decision surprising, to say the least.

And it obviously shocked the trustees, as well, only this was not unanimous: Celia, Digby, and the priest wore frowns, while Flora and Barclay were smiling.

"See you at the meeting next week," Chad said with mock cheer.

And he was gone.

Digby growled, "That means we'll still be stuck in deadlock."

"Three for," Celia muttered, "three against."

Father Cumberbatch sighed, "And nothing in Old York will change."

The informal meeting concluded, everyone slowly filing out, except for Celia, who stayed behind to lock up.

Rather than cut across the village green to the inn, Mother and I decided to take the sidewalk, going left out of the center along Brighton Street, then right on Manchester, stopping every now and then to gaze in a storefront window.

We were crossing a narrow alley between a haberdashery and a pub when I happened to look down that alley.

Beneath a security light were Digby and

Chad, conducting their own private meeting.

A Trash 'N' Treasures Tip
Keep valuable prints and watercolor paintings where the sunlight won't fade them. This includes indirect sunlight, which, over time, can also cause damage. That's why Mother once hung her favorite watercolor in a closet, enjoying it only when she put on or hung up her clothes.

CHAPTER FOUR:
O, WHAT MAY MAN WITHIN HIM HIDE

Dearest ones!

This is Vivian (aka Mother) taking a turn at the wheel (metaphorically speaking, since I am currently navigating life's highways sans driver's license). I am thrilled to my toes that my chapter has been placed so early in this tome, allowing us to get to know each other better sooner.

Usually the chapter I've been allotted is unfairly positioned midpoint, by which time my daughter Brandy's through-her-end-of-the-telescope view of the One Who Raised Her may have unfairly colored your opinion of *moi*. She is a lovely girl, very smart, often helpful, but I'm afraid somewhat lacking in imagination.

Unfortunately, I will have to forgo my usual rebuttal of Brandy's occasionally inaccurate and often exaggerated accounts of what she terms as my "antics," because doing so would cut into my editorially imposed word count (five thousand per chapter).

I feel I must, however, sacrifice precious wordage to correct Brandy's highly exaggerated account in which she has me supposedly taking a tumble off the stage during a musical production of *Everybody Loves Opal* and getting my foot stuck in a tuba. That is patently absurd! (It was a trombone.)

It is vital, when an author is given a word count limitation, to get immediately to the point, and in order to accomplish this goal, one must carefully choose the perfect words and assemble them in just the right order.

Toward that end, I truly relish using forgotten words . . . like *inveigle, jingoistic,* and *imbroglio.* The dumbing-down of our language has resulted in a tragic loss of our syntactic heritage! You would-be writers out there, please note that I will occasionally be peppering my writing with "five-dollar" words — but not to worry! Should a meaning elude you, you need not traverse this chapter with Daniel Webster by your side — you will have Vivian Borne to guide you! To provide you change for your five.

This reminds me of the time we presented my modernization of "The Devil and Daniel Webster" at the Serenity Community Playhouse, in which I played the title role.

No, not the devil — "Diane" Webster. I must have had a dozen audience members go out of their way after to tell me they'd seen nothing like it before.

Where was I?

Yes! The need to stay on point.

Friday morning, while Brandy and Sushi slept in, I arose with the dawn and, after a Spartan (austere) breakfast of coffee and scone in the inn's dining room, I set out to perambulate (walk around) the town.

As I stepped out of the inn into the zephyr (soft, gentle breeze), our innkeeper Seabert was reconfiguring the latest prankster anagram on the outside stand. The sepulchral (gloomy) man frowned at me and remarked querulously (complaining/whining), "I'd like to get my hands on whoever keeps changing our sign."

(*Editor to Vivian:* Okay . . . this isn't working. Please stop.)

(*Vivian to Editor:* What isn't working?)

(*Editor to Vivian:* Using little-known words, then defining them parenthetically, which slows down the pace of the narrative. Also, it's condescending to the reader.)

(*Vivian to Editor:* What if I don't define the words?)

(*Editor to Vivian:* What if the reader doesn't know them?)

(*Vivian to Editor:* Now, who's being condescending?)

Well, doesn't that take the wind out of my spinnakers (sails)! I hadn't even gotten around to *inchoate, attenuate,* or *punctilious.* Well, no one can say I'm obdurate or recalcitrant. And to those of you who know the meanings of some or even all of those words, let me say (in the spirit of Old York), "Jolly good show!"

I asked Seabert, "Have you no surveillance cameras to help you catch the scallywag?"

He shook his head. "There's a village ordinance against any mounted cameras — they say it detracts from the architecture."

Had the man been more pleasant, I would gladly have informed him of the Internet spy site I frequent that specializes in tiny undetectable cameras. On the other hand, I must admit I was rather keen to see what our mysterious jokester would come up with next (inveterate Scrabble fan that I am).

So I kept that to myself and merely bid Mr. Falwell a fond farewell.

While it was too early for the shops to be open, I could think of one place certain to have its doors unlocked: the Episcopal Church. As they say, the house of God is always open for business.

When Brandy was a little girl, she and I

did a Sunday morning sampling of every church in Serenity, to give the child a broader view of the rainbow of religious possibilities. So I knew a little something about the Episcopal Church.

Organized in the States after the American Revolution, the Episcopalian sect had broken away from the Church of England, which required allegiance to the king (George III, at the time). The church might be viewed as a somewhat unlikely combination of Catholic and Protestant, retaining certain trappings of the former but embracing the latter's lack of allegiance to the pope and the ability of its clergy to marry.

Old York Episcopal was located behind the inn, just a short walking distance down a verdant path called Canterbury Lane. As the ancient stone structure came into view, nestled in a grove of thick oak trees, I took a quick intake of air. The church seemed at once sinister and beautiful — sinister by way of disrepair and decay, beautiful thanks to simplicity of design.

While I would categorize the building's architecture as Gothic — due to its tall, narrow, pointed windows and single tower with spire — its lack of ornamentation had roots in the Anglo-Saxon period. A graveyard positioned behind the church fanned out conically, older headstones in front, mostly leaning, newer ones in back.

I approached the old oaken door with its rusted hinges, gave the iron handle a tug, then stepped into a small, dark vestibule. Immediately I heard the flapping of wings — no, not angels — as a bird flew over my head, and I ducked as it soared out. I waited a moment to see if any more feathered friends might be seeking freedom before I closed the door with a thud.

A soothing male voice said, "They're coming in through the bell tower, I'm afraid. Turning into some of my most regular parishioners."

I turned to Father Cumberbatch, the handsome young priest attired in a traditional black suit with white clerical collar, not the more casual garb some younger clerics assume between services.

"I hope you don't mind, Father," I said, "my dropping by for a visit."

His smile was pleasant. "Mrs. Borne, a pleasure. Are you Episcopalian?"

As I say, in my quest for a perfect spiritual fit, I'd attended Methodist, Presbyterian, Baptist, Catholic, Episcopal, Jehovah's Witnesses, among other churches, including Serenity's synagogue. But I've never worn the label of any.

"I'm still seeking, Father. One day, perhaps, I shall find."

"Seeking is a most worthwhile pursuit." He was clearly accustomed to having a tourist stop by for a look at a house of worship right out of the English countryside. "So, then — you're here to see the church."

"No. Well, yes, of course — it's lovely. But I'm really here to see *you.*"

A curious smile formed. "Oh? Well, I'm happy to see *you,* Mrs. Borne."

"Perhaps we could sit in a pew and talk?"

"Yes. Let's."

I followed him into the church's austere interior where we sat in a hard-back pew. Down front, a scaffolding had been erected in the apse, the cracked, paint-peeling ceiling badly in need of repair.

"What's on your mind, Mrs. Borne?"

"Was Millicent Marlowe one of your parishioners?"

"Ahh . . ." He tilted his head back. "You do jump right in, don't you?"

"I'm not sure I understand, Father."

His smile was slight but winning. "Mrs. Borne, I'm well aware of your reputation for solving murders here in Serenity County. I would imagine everyone in Old York is. But I can assure you that Millie's death was just — and I don't mean to diminish it —

but just a tragic accident."

"You believe she accidentally, forgetfully, took too many pills?"

"I do, yes."

"Why, Father?"

He crossed his legs while gauging his answer.

Finally, thoughtfully, he said, "I've known Millie my whole life — I grew up here. And yes, she was a member. Very regular in her attendance. But only recently I noted a deficiency in her memory. Slightly so, but she *was* forgetting things."

"For example?"

He shrugged. "What time service is held. Now and then, she couldn't remember my name — even though, I grant you, it is unusual."

I shrugged. "Not so unusual anymore."

"Oh, you mean, the Sherlock Holmes actor? Well, with some of the younger people, maybe. Among our restrictions are indoor TV antennas, and we're still on Internet dial-up service. I'm afraid many Old Yorkians don't get around much, Mrs. Borne. We live in a kind of bubble here."

"And I take it you wouldn't mind bursting it, judging by your pro-incorporation stance on the board of trustees."

Gesturing to the scaffolding, Father Cum-

87

berbatch said tersely, "Isn't it obvious? Living in the past is one thing, but having the present crumble and fall down all around you is something else again." He sighed. "Sorry, I didn't mean to sound defensive. It's terribly limiting, having such paltry funds to make even the simplest repairs."

I nodded sympathetically. "I understand your frustration. Your church is central to the charm of this old English village, and yet the only support you have is the offering plate."

"I would be content with that," he said, twisting toward me, "if incorporation passed. It would mean growth for the town, and in turn, growth in the membership of this church."

"You might need two offering plates."

"It's not just that. The young people . . . they won't stay here. Many, perhaps most, grow up and leave as soon as they can. And what's a church without young people?"

"Eventually," I said, "it's an empty building."

"Maybe not even that, if it crumbles."

"What's your vision for the future of this church?"

"*Of course* I'm in favor of maintaining its historic look. But we need modern facilities. The idea of building even a small, new youth center, hidden away behind the church, is viewed by many in my congregation as heresy."

I gave him a gently encouraging smile. "You're a young man to be trapped in such old ways, Father. Surely you've thought of moving on."

His grin came easily. "Well, vanity is one of the seven deadly sins, and I'm afraid I committed it by jumping at the chance to have my own church at a tender age, right here where I grew up. I'm blessed to be in a faith that will allow me to get married and raise a family, which I hope to do one day. But what kind of life could I offer a wife and children on my salary, and in this dilapidated church with birds flying around?"

The heavy front door slammed shut, echoing through the sanctuary, and Fred Hackney, in paint-splattered work clothes, appeared at the end of the aisle like a confused groom.

"Sorry I'm late, Father," the man said, cap in hand, patting his comb-over back in place. "Got caught up in the doings at the theater." He smiled and nodded at me. "Hello there, Mrs. Borne. Imagine we'll be seein' you later."

"Hello, Fred. You certainly will. How are

you on this lovely morning?"

"Good as can be expected, I guess. But I'll tell you one thing — the New Vic ain't gonna be the same without Millie."

"No," I said. "I'm sure it won't. Old York was lucky to have her, and I feel denied of the chance to commune with a kindred spirit. Her like shall not pass this way again!"

Fred blinked. "Suppose not."

Father Cumberbatch said to me, "Fred's been patching up the ceiling in his spare time." Then he asked the handyman, "Do you think you can be done by Sunday's service?"

"Give 'er the ol' college try."

Yet somehow I didn't think Fred was a college man.

He was saying, "Has . . . has a date been set for the funeral?"

"Tentatively Monday," the priest said. "But I'll have more information later, after I finalize arrangements with Millie's grandson."

Fred's eyes found me. "Is there any chance rehearsal could wait till this evening, ma'am?"

My response was magnanimous. "Certainly. I know you have a lot on your plate, here and at the New Vic."

"Would seven be all right? I already put the stage manager and lighting technician on standby."

"Seven will be just fine," I said. "Thank you for your efficiency and hard work, Fred."

"Okeydokey, Mrs. Borne. See you then."

And the handyman continued down the aisle toward the scaffolding.

Father Cumberbatch rose from the pew with a tight smile. "I suppose I should get to work, too. If there's nothing else, Mrs. Borne, I'll take my leave. I have Millie's eulogy to prepare."

I stood, put a hand to my chest and assumed a spiritual gaze. "Is it permissible for me to stay on for a few moments?"

"You're always a welcome guest in the Lord's house," he said warmly.

As Father Cumberbatch headed off somewhere, I wandered down to have a look at the altar, going as far as the scaffolding would allow. Fred was up on the wooden platform, applying a plaster patch to the dome ceiling, much as I do for my bunions, and I watched for a minute or two. Fred was methodical but not slow, a first-rate patcher-upper.

I called, "Will you finish today, do you think?"

He gazed down at me. "With the plaster, yup. But I gotta come back tomorrow to paint it."

"You know what would be wonderful? A ceiling mural! It would give people something to look at during the sermon." Counting organ pipes gets old.

"I'm not *that* kind of painter," he said.

"Well, I didn't really think you were. It was just an idea. Anyway, I don't imagine the church could afford a really nice mural like that."

"I dunno. Might be able to now."

"Oh?"

Fred squatted on his scaffold and wiped excess plaster from the trowel with a rag. "Yup. Millie left considerable money to the church. In her will."

"Well, what a lovely bequest! How much exactly?" My neck was aching from craning up, but such are the sacrifices of crime detection.

"Not sure, Mrs. Borne. I only know because I accidentally overheard a little somethin', when she was telling Chad about it."

"How did that go over with her grandson?"

"Chad about blew a gasket. The boy was *not* pleased."

"Perhaps he's not Episcopalian."

"I don't think he's anything at all, exceptin' a pain in the . . . somethin' you don't mention in church."

So Millie had left the church a substantial amount. Interesting.

"What about Father Cumberbatch?" I asked. "Is he aware of the bequest?"

"That I can't tell you."

The young cleric hadn't *seemed* to know about it. Or had he just been playing his cards close to his collar?

From above came a voice — not a heavenly one, just Fred's: "Look, Mrs. Borne, I probably shouldn't even've mentioned it."

"Not to worry, dear, my lips are sealed, and your words are in the vault." That was a mixed metaphor, but what did a handyman know about metaphors? "Besides, the will's contents will soon become public knowledge."

"I guess. Not my business. Why are you interested? Out-of-towner and all."

"Oh, I just like to fit in wherever I go. See you at seven!"

My next stop was the Old York Museum, ostensibly to learn more about the history of the village, but in reality to seek owner Barclay Starkadder's thoughts on Millie's supposedly failing faculties.

Located on Cambridge, the museum was

a large three-story redbrick English baroque house with a central triangular pediment at its top, hipped roof dormers, and rows of white-painted sash windows. Sweeping steps led up to a stone porch with an intricately carved walnut door, attached to which was a brass plate, reading HOURS: TUES-SAT, 10AM-5PM. SUN 2PM-6PM. CLOSED MONDAYS.

The entrance was unlocked and I stepped into a foyer onto an industrial-type mat as a bell over the door rang shrilly, making me jump a trifle. An oriental carpet-runner guided me into a grand central hallway overseen by a sparkling antique crystal chandelier and a massive walnut grandfather clock, its brass pendulum swinging slowly. On the walls hung gilt-framed oil portraits of long-departed Old Yorkians, their stern eyes appraising me.

Find me lacking if you like, fellas, I thought. *I'm here and you're gone!*

To my left was a parlor fully furnished in the baroque period — ornate couches and chairs of walnut and ebony, plush Persian rugs, green velvet curtains with tasseled draw backs, gilded mirrors, and expensive wall tapestries. A red velvet rope drawn across the threshold prevented a more thorough inventory of the room. I felt as if

I'd just entered the residence of English nobility — a duke, let's say, circa Queen Anne.

To my right was a library, also cordoned off, with floor-to-ceiling bookcases housing a vast collection of leather-bound volumes. A grand piano dominated one end, while a huge fireplace (unlit) consumed the other, around which clustered an assortment of ornately carved chairs in the Tudor and Georgian styles.

One could imagine my imaginary handsome duke seated before a roaring fire, enjoying his pipe and brandy, a Great Dane slumbering at his feet, as an expensive Edison phonograph played Beethoven's Piano Concerto no. 5 in E-flat Major, entitled *Emperor* — but perhaps I've gone too far.

As I stood agape in the grand hall, stunned by the opulence around me, a rustling sound drew my attention down the corridor leading to the back of the house.

A woman seemed to be floating toward me. Her blue eighteenth-century floor-length gown, its taffeta material the source of rustling, had a voluminous skirt, tight bodice, high lace neck, and full sleeves. Beneath a large black hat with plumes, the woman's raven hair cascaded in ringlets to slender shoulders.

Is this the ghost of the mistress of the manor?

The apparition spoke. "Welcome. I'm Brenda Starkadder. I'm assistant curator here at the museum."

"Thank heavens. For a moment I thought I'd encountered a spectral spirit."

Her laugh had a snort in it that brought the moment down to earth. "That's rather the intended effect. But sometimes I startle patrons, in my vintage attire and wig." She shrugged. "It's part of the attraction."

As lovely as her costume was, Brenda herself was certainly *not* the attraction. Terming her features as plain would be kind: protruding brown eyes, wide nose, thin lips, weak chin. I guessed her age at about forty.

"Dear, may I assume your father is Barclay Starkadder, the curator?"

"If you do, you'll be wrong. Barclay's my uncle. My parents are no longer living."

"How terribly sad. Does your uncle own the museum?"

"No. The house and antiquities belonged to one of the trustees who left everything to the town, but our family has managed it for years."

I smiled and raised a forefinger. " 'There have always been Starkadders at Cold

96

Comfort Farm!' "

The bulging eyes blinked. "Pardon?"

"The book? Stella Gibbons? The movie? Kate Beckinsale? Anything ring a bell?"

"I'm afraid not. But I can tell you one thing."

"Please do."

"There *have* always been Starkadders in Old York."

Perhaps she was, as our Brit cousins say, having a laugh; but I did not pursue it. Instead I gestured to the grand staircase. "Where do those lovely steps lead? Obviously the second floor, but what will I find there?"

She pointed up. "A variety of British artifacts dating back to the seventeen hundreds. Top floor is closed off. If those stairs present a problem, ma'am, there are steps in back with a stair-lift."

"Very thoughtful of you, dear, but I'm not an invalid just yet! Is your uncle around?"

"No, but he should be here any moment."

I folded my hands at my bosom and smiled at her. "When he arrives, would you be so kind as to inform him that Vivian Borne would like a moment of his valuable time?"

"Of course."

The bell over the door made me jump

97

again, as a group of tourists entered. Brenda floated off to greet them. Such a lovely dress! Such a drab wearer. She was a figure out of Henry James, a spinster dolled up for nobody.

I headed up the staircase, finding myself tuckered at the top. After my gentle protest that I was not an invalid, I almost wished I'd taken that stair-lift.

Catching my breath, I wandered into the first of four rooms that yawned open off the wide wood-gleaming hallway. Here, a series of glass-top cases displayed the town's history: old faded photographs of the first trustees, early life in the village, the original town charter.

The second room contained manikins, male and female alike, dressed in period clothing. More display cases held other vintage fashion items, such as women's handbags and hair ornaments, and men's fobs and watches.

The third room I granted only a cursory look, where a panoply of weapons under glass were not as appetizing as pheasant (under glass?) (get it?). But even a glimpse revealed an impressive array of old pistols, rifles, swords, and daggers.

The fourth room was more to my taste, with its vast array of china, pottery, silver tea sets, and so forth. While some antiques were under lock and key, many were arranged on wall shelves behind velvet ropes.

One shelf of delicate china caught my eye, and I approached as close as I could, squinting at a compendium of Chelsea Red and Brown Anchor plates (so noted on white placards).

"Quite lovely, aren't they?" a deeply sonorous male voice intoned behind me.

I turned, mildly startled. Possibly with the tiniest jump.

Barclay Starkadder, well-trimmed beard and graying temples, might have been the dapper ghost of the older John Barrymore, before the great actor's decline by drink had gotten too out of hand, at least. Unlike his niece, however, this Starkadder was no walking museum display, his three-piece brown tweed suit decidedly twenty-first century.

"Quite lovely indeed," I said, with just a touch of my posh English accent (Brandy wasn't around, so I could get away with classing things up a bit). I pointed to an unusual pair of cups and saucers. "And what can you tell me about those? I can't read the card from here."

"They're *actually* Derby chocolate cups — hence no handles — and Trembleuse saucers, circa 1794. The female paintings on the cups were done by Richard Askew. The background design on each is puce mark and crossed baton dots."

What an impressive authority. What a resonant voice. What a pompous arse.

I said, "Simply exquisite. I *do* hope everything is well insured."

He ignored my question, which I admit was perhaps a tad gauche. "Welcome to our modest offering, Mrs. Borne. My niece said you wished to speak to me . . . ?"

"Yes, actually. I wanted to know if you thought Millie's death was accidental."

"Where in England are you from originally?" he asked with a frown. "I can't place your accent."

I was not about to let him change the subject. "Millie's death? Do you think it was an unintentional overdose of medication?"

An eyebrow rose. He had an overly theatrical way about him that rubbed me wrong. He said, "Certainly you're not implying anything *untoward*?"

"If by 'untoward' you mean, do I think Millie was murdered, *yes* . . . I'm implying something very untoward happened."

"Why on earth, madam, would you make such an assumption?"

I raised an eyebrow. "I make such an assumption because of the obvious tension on display at the meeting last night between the two pro and con factions, regarding incorporation of your village."

The frown deepened. "Balderdash, woman. You make it sound like our meeting was obstreperous! The very idea that one of us would harm another who held a different viewpoint is utterly fatuous, and I refuse to palaver any further along such amphigoric lines."

(*Editor to Vivian:* I trust you are accurately reporting what Mr. Starkadder said and are not taking this opportunity to show off your own vocabulary. If so, please edit.)

(*Vivian to Editor:* I swear to you that this is verbatim. My memory is highly implacable, and I would never attempt to pull off such a transparent cozenage.)

I asked, "How do *you* stand on incorporation?"

He pursed his lips. "Let's just say I am quite content with the status quo."

"So you vote no, then. And your niece — Brenda? What might her position be?"

Barclay shrugged elaborately. "Frankly, we've never discussed it. And, one day, when she takes my place on the board, my niece can vote as she pleases. One can only hope that one has set an example, where honoring the past, and maintaining its virtues, are concerned. Now, madam, if you'll excuse me . . . I have much to do."

He turned brusquely and walked away.

I lingered, mulling over our conversation while pretending to study a mahogany tea box with copper bands, its placard saying it dated to the year of the Boston Tea Party.

Fighting a sudden craving for tea, I departed the museum, took a left and walked half a block to a two-story Tudor-style brick building whose window quietly said, LANCASTER REALTY & LAND DEVELOPMENT. This was before business hours, but the door was open, which I always take as an invitation.

The interior made no particular attempt to invoke the English village theme — a receptionist's metal desk, vacant, a few straight-back chairs along the walls and lots of framed pictures (with written descriptions beneath) of properties in Old York.

The door to the office beyond was shut.

I knocked.

"Yes?" came an impatient, borderline nasty male voice.

"Mr. Lancaster? Vivian Borne. Might I have a word?"

A long pause preceded the eventual, "Come in, come in."

I did so and took the waiting client chair. Digby Lancaster, who did not rise, was in a rust-color sports jacket over a green polo shirt, a considerable contrast to Barclay Starkadder's three-piece suit. He was plump and pale and his hair was cut short, as if perhaps his barber of choice was at a military base; his bulldog features made no attempt to compose themselves pleasantly for me.

"Something I can do for you, Mrs. Borne?"

"Well, first let me thank you for allowing the show to go on," I said. "Judging by your attitude at the board meeting, I thought you might be a naysayer."

He shrugged. "When you're outnumbered, why not be generous? I'm sure you'll do fine. I'll be there. It's kind of required."

I smiled through the insult. "Well, a lot is required in Old York, isn't it?"

He rolled his eyes. "Tell me about it."

"Have you lived in the village long, Mr. Lancaster?"

"I grew up here, and I got out in a hurry."

"What brought you back, if I might ask?"

He shrugged. "My dad passed on and left me property."

"How much property? Again, if I might be so bold."

"I own a number of buildings, and some undeveloped land. And, of course, I'm a realtor. I do all right. I could do better."

"You mean, if incorporation came in."

He shrugged, but then nodded. "This little bump in the road is a potential gold mine. Tourists eat this kind of stuff up. I have some land on the outskirts but within the village territory, as defined in our charter." He shook his head. "Oh, what I could *do* with that hunk of real estate, given half a chance."

"What could you do with it," I asked gently, "given half a chance?"

He smiled, the bulldog happily going after the bone I'd tossed. "Imagine a big motel playin' up this Brit angle. Imagine a strip mall with English-type names for the stores, you know, Ye Olde Smoke Shop, Ye Olde Launderette, Henry the Eighth Burgers, that kind of thing. But a lot of these locals wouldn't stoop over to pick up money in the street."

I shook my head sadly. "They're misguided, Mr. Lancaster. Progress is always inevitable."

"Isn't that the truth."

"You must have been surprised to hear Chad say he intended to honor his grandmother's wishes and vote against incorporation."

"Uh, yeah. That was disappointing, all right."

I smiled innocently. "Is that what you were telling him last night? I noticed you two talking, after the meeting."

He got even paler. "That was nothing. I was just giving him my, you know, condolences."

"Did you know Millicent well?"

"Not really. I've only been back a year. She was one of those theatrical types, you know, one of those small-town divas. Kind of pitiful but harmless."

That was certainly not called for, but I did not react. Acting is largely reacting; but not when you're grilling a suspect in a murder case. Speaking of which . . .

"Do you buy that Millie's death was accidental, Mr. Lancaster? Doesn't it seem awfully convenient, coming when it does?"

He pawed the air. "I don't mean to sound callous, Mrs. Borne, but it's not coincidental or shocking or anything else for a senior citizen to pass away."

"Is that what you were doing? Waiting for her to pass away?"

He frowned. I'd revealed too much.

"Lady, I have things to do. I'll see you at

the play Saturday night. You break a leg, okay? Break a couple."

His smile was ghastly, but I did smile back, and got quickly out of there.

I made my way across the village green — where volunteers were making preparations for tomorrow afternoon's fete — intending to drop in on Flora Payton at her floral shop on Manchester.

As I entered, a little bell above the door tinkled (and I didn't jump at all, thank you), and I found Flora arranging a vase of red roses behind the counter. She was wearing another low-cut top, pink, her red hair caressing her shoulders.

"Well, hello," she said, looking up. "Vivian, isn't it?"

"It is Vivian," I replied, closing the door, the bell sounding again. "And you're Flora."

She grinned. "And I'm Flora."

"Might I say that you're looking just as lovely as those blossoms." A little flattery does wonders to loosen Ye Olde Tongues.

"Why thank you, Vivian. May I help you?"

I've also found that greasing a palm can prove an effective loosening agent, tongue-wise. "I'd like to purchase a cheery bouquet to brighten up my room."

"I'm sure we can find something to do just the trick. Anything in mind?"

"What do you suggest, dear?"

Setting the roses aside, Flora came out from behind the counter, revealing the rest of her ensemble: a tight black skirt and red kitten heels. Unlike her flowers, this child bloomed all year long.

"These are quite lovely," she said, gesturing to a vase of orange roses and lilies. "I call that *Clockwork Orange.*" Flora gestured to another vase brimming with pink roses and carnations. "Or perhaps you'd prefer *Pretty in Pink.*" She giggled. "I name all of my arrangements after movies."

"I gathered that, dear," I allowed. "Quite clever. I'll take *Pretty in Pink.*"

I once attended a theatrical showing of *A Clockwork Orange,* just getting in out of the rain, and in fact went in humming "Singin' in the Rain," which as a song has never quite worked as well for me since. But back to our story.

"I'll wrap it up," Flora said, reaching for the pink concoction.

Following her back to the counter, I eased into the purpose of my visit. "I visited the museum, earlier. It's really quite impressive."

She was wrapping the arrangement in cellophane. "Yes, certainly is."

"I understand the town actually owns the

107

artifacts and that grand old house itself."

"That's right." She was tying the cellophane top with a pink ribbon.

"Something I can't quite grasp."

"Oh?"

"If Barclay Starkadder is a paid employee, not an owner, why ever would *he* be against incorporation?"

She took her eyes off my purchase. "Well, that's easily answered. He gets his salary from a trust fund set up by the founding families, years ago. If this town square became Tourist Central, the museum could be moved to a smaller location, and that 'grand house' used for something far more profitable."

"Ah. I would think, after incorporation, the contents of the museum might even be liquidated, those valuable antiques sold to fund civic improvements."

"Wouldn't be surprised, Vivian. And it would almost certainly put Barclay out of a cushy job."

"I see. And you, dear? How do you stand on the incorporation issue?"

"That's easily answered, too. I vote no. I understand progress and all that. But me? I couldn't possibly compete against a chain, or some big supermarket that carried flowers."

"Might I pose one last question, dear?"

"Sure."

"Do you agree with those who insist that Millie took an accidental overdose?"

Even frowning in thought she was a pretty thing. "I'm not sure, Vivian. But I did see her Thursday morning at the theater, about an order for flowers. And she took a pill right in front of me."

"When was this, dear?"

"Oh. Around eleven."

Chad said she'd taken one earlier.

She was frowning again. "Are you all right, Vivian?"

"Fine, dear. What do I owe you?"

"Fifty-one fifty." She grinned. "That's dollars, not pounds."

Thank goodness not *everything* here was British!

I walked back to the inn, where the standing sign had once again been tampered with: DEATH COMES TO ONE MORE NO.

MOTHER'S
TRASH 'N' TREASURES TIP

When traveling abroad, you may spot a lovely antique that seems a real bargain. But before purchasing your precious discovery, make sure you know that country's regulations on exporting goods, or you may take home a fine as well as a find.

CHAPTER FIVE:
SO FOUL AND FAIR A DAY I
HAVE NOT SEEN

Brandy here. Did everyone make it through Mother's chapter unscathed? Anyone need an aspirin break? A visit with Captain Morgan? No? Then onward.

Friday morning I slept till ten, then had a late breakfast in the dining room at the Horse and Groom, barely making the 11 A.M. cut-off. Mother joined me midway and, over a scone and tea, filled me in on what you've just heard from her.

"Mother," I said, "you're really jumping the gun here. There's every reason to think Millie either accidentally overdosed or simply had a heart attack. Especially since Flora says that she saw Millie take an extra pill Thursday morning."

"But it still *could* be murder."

"It's a possibility, and in this climate of dispute over incorporation, maybe a good possibility. But shouldn't we wait to see what the coroner back in Serenity has to say? And if it *is* murder, Sheriff Rudder will swoop down with deputies and we can go on about the very important business of putting on your play tomorrow evening."

All right, that last part was pandering. When all else fails with Mother, push the theater button.

"Dear, haven't we been at this long enough for you to know how vital it is to get cracking in a murder investigation? Do you know the statistics?"

"What statistics?"

She raised a lecturing forefinger. "How about this one: with every hour that passes after a murder, the perpetrator's odds of getting away with it multiply tenfold."

"Where did you get that one?"

"Well, I didn't get it anywhere. It's common sense."

I nibbled on my last piece of crispy bacon. Well, I was saving one piece for Sushi up in the room.

"Mother," I said, "common sense is that we enjoy this beautiful little displaced English village. We shop. We have mid-afternoon tea and crumpets, whatever *they* are, then come back and relax before to-night's crucial dress rehearsal."

The theater button again.

My tactic worked, to some degree anyway.

Her concession was that we would interrupt our shopping afternoon with a visit to the New Vic — not to prep for dress, but to chat with Chad.

"This sounds," I said, "suspiciously like more before-the-fact murder investigation."

"That will be the subtext, dear. But there's another matter we need to attend to. We dodged a bullet last night, you know."

"Did we?"

She nodded several times. "Millie died before I had a chance to get our contract signed for the Scottish play. Fortunately, the board's vote to put it on will box young Chad Marlowe into a corner. The show will go on! Just as Millie's last words bade us do."

She was starting to believe Millie really had said that.

The theater doors were unlocked and we crossed the empty lobby, taking the turn down the vending machine hallway, where we found Chad's door open. He didn't see us at first, but we saw him, all right.

In the black suit again but with the tie MIA and his collar unbuttoned, the long-haired artistic director of the New Vic was seated behind his desk and leaning forward, smiling up at a black-haired girl. She wore a black T-shirt with long ragged sleeves, a short black skirt, and clunky hardware-heavy boots. Her lipstick and eye shadow were black, her face pale with white powder, eyebrows, nose, and lower lip pierced. Though she looked like death warmed over, she was laughing.

And so was Chad.

The Goth girl had one foot lifted behind her and her pink pierced tongue was flicking over black lips.

Mother knocked hard on the open door. *"I beg pardon!"*

They were startled. We might have caught them at much worse than just flirting across a desk, the way they reacted.

"Chad," Mother said, "I don't mean to interrupt. . . ."

What else could she have been meaning to do?

". . . but I need a word or two on several key matters." She gestured back to the corridor. "My daughter and I can wait until your meeting is over, if you like."

Chad's embarrassed surprise morphed into irritation and then finally into an unconvincing smile. "Mrs. Borne, Glenda and I were just going over some details about tomorrow night's performance."

Glenda's surprise had become that special sullenness reserved for anyone older than

114

her. "I run the box office," she said.

Mother beamed. "Well, I hope to keep your little hands busy! Let's rub those pretty black nails of yours pink!"

Glenda's eyes opened wide and stayed that way as they traveled sideways to the seated Chad, who shrugged.

"I think we have everything in place, Glenda," Chad said. "We'll talk later."

She gave him a "whatever" nod and brushed by us.

I nodded to Chad, as we took chairs across from him, but he didn't acknowledge me.

Mother, holding on to her purse like something keeping her afloat, leaned forward and said, "And how are you holding up, dear boy?"

His expression turned somber. "It's difficult to believe Grandmother is gone." He gestured around the small office with its many framed posters of Millie's Shakespearean productions here at the New Vic over the decades. "She *was* this theater. I could never hope to replace her."

"Well, dear, does that mean you're not going to try? You're not thinking of *closing* the theater, are you? Are you perhaps thinking of selling it?"

The barrage of questions made him wince.

"Frankly, Mrs. Borne, I haven't got that far in my thinking yet. Right now I just want to get your production up and running, and when the curtain comes down . . . we'll see."

"Is that what you were discussing with Mr. Lancaster last night?"

That stopped him like a slap. Now he wore no expression at all. "No. Digby was just expressing his condolences, as you might expect."

"Yes, he does seem like a lovely, caring man. We spoke this morning, you know."

"Yes."

Mother smiled. "Oh, you *did* know?"

"No, I mean, I was just . . . what can I do for you, Mrs. Borne?"

Mother took a beat. "Before her tragic passing, *right* before actually, your grandmother said the contract for my performance was waiting in this office. I really should sign it, you know. Just a matter of form . . . no pun intended!"

She was overplaying, but then when wasn't she?

But there was no problem. Chad knew right where the contract was, among several small stacks of papers, and Mother signed with a flourish, keeping a copy for herself.

"Now if you would like to give me a check," she said as offhandedly as she could manage (not very), "you won't even have to fuss with it after the performance."

He smirked at her. "No, Mrs. Borne. I think that can wait. I'll pay you promptly after the show."

"No problem!" She got to her feet, clutching her purse. "Always glad to sing for my supper!"

Chad gave me a look and I gave him a shrug — our only exchange in this conversation.

In the hallway, Mother said, "That young woman he was talking to? Glenda? That was no good witch."

"She's just a Goth girl, Mother."

"I think she would make a wonderful suspect!"

I frowned at her. "You do? Why? What's her motive?"

"Oh, I have no idea. I was thinking more in terms of . . . casting."

The dress rehearsal Friday night did not go well, not only because I mixed up the hats I handed Mother from the wings, but because she uncharacteristically went up on her lines during Macbeth's famous soliloquy that begins, "Tomorrow and tomorrow and tomorrow . . ." She said "tomorrow" maybe twelve times before getting back on track.

Normally she can repeat that thing in her sleep (and often does).

I had no excuse for my prop blunders, but I think Mother was distracted by her possible murder case. The number of pills that Millie may or may not have taken remained unknown, if you considered the data Mother had gathered came from murder suspects (and better ones than Glenda).

At any rate, I was confident that at the actual performance, with an audience present, Mother would rise to the occasion with her usual effervescence, and hopefully not give too semaphoric a performance. (The end of *my* big words for this chapter.)

Saturday morning — the day of the fete — the aroma (and clatter) of breakfast being served in the dining room below stirred me. Then Sushi's cold nose roused me to full wakefulness, more or less, the little mutt having decided I'd (we'd) slept enough.

After a quick shower in the tiny bathroom, I put on an outfit befitting an English fete — or anyway my idea of one: tailored slacks, button-down Oxford shirt, and an argyle cardigan.

I fed Soosh, gave her an injection, took her outside via the back stairway to do her business, returned her to the room, then knocked on Mother's door.

Getting no response, I headed down to breakfast.

Mother, in yet another Breckenridge slacks outfit (orange), was seated at a table for two beneath a print (faded) of a stable boy grooming a horse. She waved to get my attention, as if she might be hard to spot, and I wove through the crowded room, the inn having filled up with tourists overnight. The fete was drawing a crowd already.

Both Seabert (ill-fitting gray suit) and Celia (outdated purple dress with shoulder pads) were tending to the diners, aided by a single young server. Seabert worked hard to take orders and keep the water, coffee, and tea flowing, as attested by the sweat beaded on his brow.

Celia, ever the congenial if insincere hostess, flitted among the tables, asking if anyone needed anything — and if they did, ordering her husband to perform the task.

Seabert came over to us. "We've got kippers with scrambled eggs and black pudding . . . or you can have porridge."

Since I didn't like smoked herring, and Mother warned me about black pudding (look it up), I asked for scrambled eggs only. Mother ordered the porridge knowing I'd walk out on her if she had the black pudding.

After Seabert departed, Mother asked me, "When's that delightful police chief of yours joining us?"

"Around noon."

"How lovely."

I frowned at her. "Mother, you aren't planning to bother Tony about this Millie thing, are you?"

"Of course not, dear. It's not Chief Cassato's business. Strictly Sheriff Rudder's bailiwick. On the other hand, it never hurts to have an expert's opinion, does it?"

After the rehearsal debacle last night, Tony and I had talked on our cells for a half hour — unusual for the tight-lipped copper — and were both looking forward to attending the fete together.

Mother said ominously, "I have a bad feeling about today, darling, that I just can't seem to shake."

"Can't or don't want to?"

She gestured dramatically. "No matter how sunny a day we may have out there, I fear a dark cloud is hovering over the little village of Old York."

Oh brother.

"Nonsense," I said. "It's going to be a great day."

"I don't think so, dear. *Both* bunions are bothering me."

"That's because you walked all over town yesterday. Plus, there was the rehearsal."

"What about that message, on our doorstep? 'Death comes to one more no'?"

I had to admit that was unsettling. Before, it had been a practical joker's fun, seemingly, with the innocuous messages of "rotten room," and "horses on the moon." Now we had an apparent threat to the remaining anti-incorporation board members.

"Flora Payton, Barclay Starkadder, and maybe Chad," I said. "Are they in danger? Should we call Sheriff Rudder?"

"He's not taking my calls."

Seabert dropped off our hot tea and gave us a smile that was more like a crack in his face. Then he was gone.

I leaned in. "Mother, could we please, please, *please* just have a nice day?"

Her sigh came up from her toes (or maybe bunions). "I will do my best, dear."

"And please don't mention that latest sidewalk sign to Tony or get into any of this. He's my date, not your sounding board."

"I wouldn't *dream* of ruining your day," she said. "Why should a little murder get in the way of your fun?"

"Mother . . ."

She sighed. "We'll have a wonderful day."

"Thank you."

But I was starting to dread what might be a fete worse than death.

Our breakfasts arrived, and while we ate, Mother's spirits lifted as she told me in detail about the priceless antiquities she'd seen at the museum, her earlier account having focused strictly on her encounters with suspects.

With our meal finished, we were enjoying a second cup of tea when the patrons in the dining room began to stir, their faces turning to the front windows.

I could hear the muffled sound of bagpipes.

"What's going on?" I asked an older couple at the next table.

"The parade is about to start," the woman replied.

"There is one?"

The man explained, "There's always a parade before the fete begins."

Mother beamed at them. "I love a parade!" For a terrible moment, I feared she might break into song.

"Well, if you want to see it, you'd better hurry," the man said, signing his breakfast bill to his room. "It only goes around the square once."

As the diners began abandoning their tables, I told Mother I'd meet her in front of the inn, then hurried back to my room to get Sushi, knowing she would enjoy the spectacle.

Back when Soosh was blind, I would lug her along with me, strapped to my chest in a leopard-print baby sling, and I'd brought that carrier knowing I'd be taking her to the fete — better than putting her on a leash where the little mutt could get herself stepped on. (So from now until the end of this chapter, just remember that the little fur ball is affixed to my front like a cute fuzzy goiter.)

Soon, beneath a bright blue sky, Sushi and I joined Mother on a curb already lined with tourists and locals alike, just as the band of bagpipe players in uniforms (not kilts, darn) marched playing a Scottish tune.

Next came a half-dozen men wearing white shirts, green vests, black short pants, high white socks, and black shoes, each holding a stick in his hand. What was that about?

Mother answered my unspoken question, shouting right in my ear: "They're called Morris dancers, dear!"

What *didn't* that woman know?

The green-vested six stopped for a minute

123

to perform a folk dance, hopping and skipping and tapping the sticks together, the bells strapped to their shins jingling. It was at once absurd and exhilarating and impressive.

Following the Morris dancers were two floats, one arrayed with people dressed in medieval costumes and, in the other, folks in colonial attire. Court jesters and Pilgrims walked alongside their respective floats, throwing small candies into the crowd.

Bringing up the rear was a vintage white Cadillac convertible driven by Digby Lancaster, wearing a nice suit and tie for a change. Seated next to him was Celia Falwell, in her best out-of-fashion frock, and in back, Flora Paxton in a low-cut dress sandwiched between Father Cumberbatch and an impeccable Barclay Starkadder.

The trustees waved royally to the crowd as the car crawled by. Most bystanders smiled and waved back, while others stood stony faced, even frowning; not all the subjects in the little kingdom of Old York seemed happy.

As the parade concluded, the crowd en masse began to move toward the village green for the fete, a tide that swept Mother and me (and Sushi) along.

We stepped onto grass that couldn't have

been greener in 1950s Technicolor, while vivid banners strung between poles around the perimeter flapped in the cool autumn breeze, as if waving hello, and an orchestra in the band shell welcomed one and all by striking up a lively march.

While Mother and I began to wander the colorful tents and open tables — each offering a game or event for a modest fee — I received a text from Tony telling me he'd arrived and was waiting at the fortune-teller's booth.

Mother raised a finger to her lips. "Just imagine our chief of police having his fortune told. *That* I would love to see, and hear."

"You're welcome to come along. Murder-talk isn't."

"Thank you, but no, dear. There's a table selling antiques that I'd like to check out."

And Mother struck out on her own. Always a relief — at first.

Tony, casually dressed in a sport coat, polo shirt, and jeans on a rare day off, was waiting in front of a red and white striped tent, a sign above its entrance reading: HILDA'S HOUSE OF FORTUNES, $5.00.

We kissed briefly, an attention-seeking Sushi trying to insert her nose between us.

"All right, okay," Tony laughed, petting

125

her head. "I'm glad to see you, too."

"Can you stay over?" I asked.

He shook his head. "Sorry, I have to be back this evening. I have three men out sick. Something going around."

Hiding my disappointment, I squeezed his arm. "Well, we'll always have Paris . . . and this afternoon. Come on, let's hear what Hilda has to say about what the future holds."

"I'm going to guess the future has a woman with oversize eyeglasses in it."

"Well, let's see what else it holds."

"Why not?"

We were the first to enter the tent, where a woman in her seventies decked out in garish gypsy garb, head scarf, earrings and all, sat at a little cloth-draped table, a crystal ball in its center.

With a bony, ring-encrusted hand, she gestured to a single folding chair in front of her, which I took, Tony standing beside me.

"I am called Hilda," she declaimed with a melodramatic intensity worthy of Mother. "Your *hand,* my child."

I held it out and her bony grasp settled around it, firm but gentle. She closed her eyes, opened them, then released my hand.

"Before year's end," she pronounced, "your sweet little one there will have a brother."

I gestured to Sushi. "Ah . . . this isn't a baby. It's a dog."

She leaned forward, squinting. "Thank the stars! I feared you had brought me the hairiest baby in creation."

I looked up at Tony, whose smile was doing its best to hold back a chuckle.

The gypsy went on. "My vision is flawed — that is, the vision of my eyes." As an aside, in a voice drained of melodrama, she added, "Normally I wear glasses, but they take the edge off my costume." The melodramatic tone returned. "Let me consult the crystal ball. . . ."

That she could see. Well, it was a good size.

Hilda peered into the glass. She frowned.

"You will soon be in grave danger," foretold the gypsy.

"I was kind of hoping for riches beyond my wildest dreams."

"Aren't we all, my dear. But heed these words: beware the Cyclops!"

I frowned. "The only Cyclops I know is in that *Sinbad* movie."

Hilda sighed deeply and sat back, exhausted. A one-minute reading really took it out of the old gal. "I'm sorry, the vision has faded."

"Okay, well, good to know. I'll keep my

eye out for a Cyclops!" Nobody laughed — including you.

I looked up at Tony. "Your turn."

"Think I'll take a pass," he said, not amused by this experience.

When I tried to pay Hilda her five-dollar fee, she waved two bony hands and said, "I will take no profit for ill fortune."

Outside the tent, I said, "Okay, *that* was weird. Well, as monsters in Ray Harry-hausen movies go, the Cyclops is better than Hydra or the Troglodyte."

"Who's Ray Harry What's-It?"

"He did the best monsters. Tony, we may not be cut out for each other after all. Not if you don't love old movies, too."

"I'm willing to be schooled, if you provide the popcorn."

"Deal." We were strolling. "I wonder what *your* fortune would have been?"

Tony slipped an arm around my shoulders. "I already found my fortune," he said, and kissed my cheek. "How would you like me to win you a prize at one of these booths?"

I kissed his cheek. "I already won the big prize."

We'll pause now for everyone to feel just a little sick.

Then I said, "But win me something anyway. Let's start with the Coconut Shy."

"What the heck is that?"

The idea behind the Coconut Shy game (I get the coconut part, but not the shy) was to try to knock the hard round fruit off posts with a wooden ball. Sounded simple, but the coconuts were in wire holders and not so easily dislodged, as was attested by a twenty-something man whose three throws bounced off the coconuts and went into the back netting.

"Sorry young man," said a mustachioed middle-aged barker sporting a candy-striped apron. "Anyone else? Three balls for ten dollars!"

I whispered to Tony, "That's a pretty high tariff. If you back out, I won't think any less of you."

"How much less do you think of me now?"

I fake-punched his arm.

Tony motioned to the barker, who came over, collected my guy's engraving of Alexander Hamilton, then handed him the first wooden ball.

Tony wound up for the pitch, fired the ball, and struck out. Ditto for the second ball. But the third one — wow! — knocked a coconut off its post, along with the metal holder. My police chief always packs guns, even when he goes out unarmed.

The prize was a little stuffed bear, which

Sushi immediately claimed for herself, and I tucked it in the pouch with her.

"What's next?" asked a puffed-up Tony.

"There's something called Wiggly Wire that looks interesting," I replied, having noticed the game earlier. "Don't get too cocky. It's tough, too."

"Lead the way."

The crowd was getting thick now, and Tony and I held hands as we wove in and around people. As we walked by the Jumble tent (donated clothing for sale), I noticed Celia and Father Cumberbatch standing to one side, in conference. I just happened to catch a snippet of their conversation.

"How *much*?" the priest was asking.

"Twenty thousand *each*," the innkeeper replied.

"I couldn't pay that if I wanted to!"

And that was all I heard . . . though it might be enough.

In the game of Wiggly Wire, a contestant tries to pass a metal ring along a twisting wire without touching the ring to the wire and thereby setting off a disqualifying buzzer (a variation on the board game Operation). The line looked endless, so Tony and I watched for a few minutes, then moved on.

At the first-aid tent, Tony stopped in to

give a professional hello to the two para-medics — male and female — who were on hand in the event of a medical emergency. They worked out of Serenity and he knew them both.

While waiting outside, I spotted Flora and Digby near the band shell, also in confer-ence — or rather, having an obvious dis-agreement.

The florist pointed a finger in the realtor's face, to which he gave her a push-away "leave me alone" gesture, then stalked off.

The surviving board members seemed an unhappy lot, at odds with their smiling, wav-ing parade appearance.

Tony emerged from the medical tent, and we began checking out other games, which seemed evenly divided between those for children (Bouncy Slide, Splat the Rat) and adults (Darts, Hoop Toss).

The big draw for adults was the Bottle Tombola, where a large crowd of over-twenty-one participants, as well as some kibitzers of any age, had gathered for the raffling off of alcoholic beverages.

Banquet-style tables had been strung together to hold several hundred bottles of beer, wine, and whiskey, each with a num-bered card taped to it. On a separate table was a colorful metal drum with crank handle, and the word *TOMBOLA!* on its front.

I heard a familiar "Oh, *you*-who!" — unmistakably Mother.

Tony and I and Sushi squeezed through the throng to reach her.

"No luck at the antiques tent?" I asked, noticing her distinct lack of packages.

"*Terribly* overpriced, dear," Mother sniffed. "But I do have tickets for the Tombola raffle."

She reached into a slacks pocket and produced them.

I started to scold her — no alcoholic beverage of any kind was to be mixed with her meds — but she broke in, "They're for *you,* dear. That time I imbibed and wound up in Kalamazoo is still fresh in my mind. I thought you might win a nice bottle of wine for you and the chief to share later."

"Well, that's very nice of you, Vivian," Tony said.

Mother handed me five tickets, each one having two numbers.

"How does this work, anyway?" I asked.

"Well, dear," Mother replied, "if the larger number on a ticket is called, you've won a bottle. The smaller number on that ticket indicates which bottle on the table is yours."

The crowd suddenly went silent as Fred

Hackney — out of his work clothes and into a sweater and slacks — stepped up to the drum, clutched the crank handle, and began to spin it, the tickets whirring inside.

Assisting Fred were local dignitaries Digby, Father Cumberbatch, and Celia.

Fred stopped cranking, opened a little door in the drum, withdrew a ticket, and handed it to Digby. Digby, in a booming voice, announced the winning number: 2,455.

A woman shrieked, rushed forward, and handed her ticket to Digby. Digby gave the woman's ticket, and the one drawn from the drum, to Father Cumberbatch, who made sure they were identical. Then the priest announced the smaller number on the tickets — 275 — and Celia found the bottle with the card 275 (white wine), which she handed ceremoniously to the excited winner.

It was a slow process, with several hundred bottles to go, meaning a long raffle.

The afternoon had become warm, which, with strapped-to-my-chest Sushi producing her own heat, was making me uncomfortable.

I asked Tony, "Mind if we go back to the inn?"

A tiny smile. "Hoping you'd ask that. I

was just starting to long for a good old-fashioned ring toss or duck pond."

I told Mother we were bailing, and tried to give her back the tickets.

Mother had a glazed look that indicated her precarious attention span was getting taxed, as well. "Dear, why don't we give them away? I'd like a little afternoon nap, what with the performance this evening."

"I'm fine with that."

She was looking around. "Oh! There's Barclay Starkadder with Brenda! I'd like to introduce you to her."

"Now?" I protested, but Mother had my arm and was dragging me away from Tony.

Soon she had inserted herself and me between the uncle and niece.

"Brenda," Mother said, having to speak up over Digby, who was announcing another winning number, "this is my daughter, Brandy."

Brenda nodded curtly. "Nice to meet you." Her eyes went to Sushi on my chest. "Cute dog. Bright-eyed."

"Yes," Mother said, "and to think she used to be blind!"

This true fact, of course, registered as a non sequitur, and put a burp in the middle of things.

Barclay, overdressed for the occasion, the

jacket of his three-piece suit folded over one arm, was ignoring us, quickly scanning the five tickets he held for the number just called.

"Damn," he said disappointedly.

"Barclay dear," Mother said, as if *dear* was the man's last name, "would you like *our* tickets? We're heading back to the inn."

"Why, thank you, Mrs. Borne." He half bowed. "Most generous, most gracious."

"Do call me Vivian," Mother purred.

"Vivian."

She pressed the tickets into the museum curator's hand. Earlier she'd told me she thought the guy was a pompous ass. But she seemed to be reconsidering that assessment.

I told both Starkadders that it was nice to meet them, then bodily steered Mother back to Tony.

"You needn't have been so rude!" she snapped.

"I wasn't rude. I said 'nice to meet you.' It just wasn't the right time for one of your lengthy conversations."

"Since when are my conversations lengthy?"

"Since . . . the dawn of time?"

She looked pointedly at Tony. "Well, Chief? What's *your* opinion?"

He was shaking his head. "Leave me out of this. Anyway, I wasn't even a witness."

A whoop went up from the crowd and we glanced over to see Barclay excitedly waving one of the tickets. He'd won a bottle, but it was as if he'd snagged a new car.

Barclay collected his prize — a bottle of beer.

"How splendid!" Mother said. "I'll wager it was one of *my* tickets. Come, let us all retire to the inn."

We were crossing the green when another shriek erupted from the Tombola crowd. This, however, was no whoop of excitement at the miracle of winning a bottle. Rather, this was a cry of alarm.

When more shouts followed, Tony sprinted in that direction.

By the time Mother and I reached the raffle crowd, Tony was ordering everyone to stand back, and as they complied, I could see Barclay, motionless on his back in the grass, and Brenda, kneeling beside her fallen uncle, pleading to the crowd and to God for help.

A TRASH 'N' TREASURES TIP
Antiques and collectibles donated to raise money for charity are often overpriced. But if you really want the item, think of the

overpayment as your contribution to the cause. Just don't try to claim it as a tax deduction, like I did.

CHAPTER SIX:
WHEN THE HURLY-BURLY'S DONE

Tony immediately went into official police mode, holding his badge high as he continued his crowd control. Someone had already summoned the paramedics, and they rushed over and pushed through, a dark-haired slender woman in her thirties and a slightly chunky redheaded male.

Mother and I were at the front and had a good view of the proceedings. As the male paramedic worked to revive Barclay, his female partner took Brenda to one side and urgently asked her, "What medications was your uncle using?"

Brenda, choking back tears, said, "Just his heart medication. . . . I don't know exactly what it is. He took it right before we left."

"Any other prescription drugs?"

Brenda shook her head. "Not that I know of."

"Over the counter?"

"Just . . . you know, simple headache

medication. Aspirin, I guess." Brenda gestured to her uncle's prone body. "He was fine until he drank that bottle of beer. Could it have reacted with the medication?"

The medic, not committing to an answer, asked, "Who's his doctor?"

Brenda gave her a name, and the medic took a few steps away and made an emergency call to the doctor for more information.

Celia, Digby, Father Cumberbatch, and Flora now gathered around Brenda, Flora slipping an arm around the woman's shoulders. Brenda turned her tear-streaked face to the florist.

"I *told* him to take that beer home and drink it there! I *told* him to take it home. It wasn't even cold!" Her words came in a near-hysterical rush. "But he wouldn't listen, said he was thirsty, just went right ahead and drank it down . . . even after I reminded him it was against the rules to drink alcohol at the fete."

"I know, honey," Flora said. "I heard you. Barclay always did think he was the exception to any rule." She said this not unkindly.

Brenda nodded, tears flowing again. "Bullheaded, that's what he is. That medication *must* have caused a bad reaction with that damn beer! If only he'd listened to me."

"Brenda," Celia said softly, "you can't be sure the beer had anything to do with . . . with what happened. Maybe it was the excitement and the heat. Anyway, blaming yourself doesn't do any good. Anyone on medication has a responsibility to —"

Brenda wasn't listening; she wasn't hearing anything now but her own sobs.

Tony was directing the crowd to get back even farther as the male paramedic placed two paddles of an automated external defibrillator against Barclay's chest, where his shirt had been opened.

A while back, since Mother was getting up there, I'd taken a course in the use of an AED device (ours was gathering dust in a closet), so I knew with each passing minute that Barclay's chances of being revived were decreasing dramatically.

"Clear," the paramedic called, then delivered Barclay a shock.

This jolt was followed by a round of chest compressions and rescue breathing, and then another shock.

Finding this difficult to watch — although Sushi was leaning out, interested in yet another inexplicable human activity — I glanced away and noticed Barclay's jacket, which had been slung over his arm, the warm weather inspiring him to take it off, as had been the case for so many fete attendees. Now it lay in a forgotten heap. I walked over, knelt as Sushi looked up at me curiously, and picked the jacket up in a half daze, just trying to be helpful somehow.

Finally, when the male paramedic ceased his efforts, he looked solemnly at Brenda, standing nearby, and shook his head, which elicited another round of tears and racking sobs from the woman.

Murmurs of shock and disbelief came in a wave from the trustees and other bystanders; then came a respectful yet ominous hush, as Father Cumberbatch knelt over Barclay, delivering a truncated version of the last rites to the deceased.

When the young priest had finished, he stood and walked slowly over to rejoin Brenda and his fellow trustees.

During all this, my eyes were mostly on Tony, who was having a low-volume conference with the two paramedics. Then he made a quick cell call. When he'd clicked off, he approached Brenda.

"I've just talked to Sheriff Rudder," Tony said, "and he's in agreement that your uncle should be taken to the hospital in Serenity."

"I don't understand," she said, blinking back tears. "Why not the funeral home in Selby? It's just fifteen miles. . . ."

"Due to the death of another trustee on Thursday," he said, "Chief Rudder has determined that there should be an autopsy."

"I still don't —"

Tony was gentle but businesslike. "Two similar deaths in three days, involving individuals with close associations — that raises questions."

Brenda, aghast, said nothing.

"*Excuse* me," Celia said, "but why should Brenda listen to you?"

"Yeah," Digby jumped in. "Just who the hell are you, buddy? I saw you flashing a badge around, but you don't work for Old York."

Nobody did. Old York didn't have any police.

Tony's badge-fold was still in his hand; he flipped it open and held it up. "Anthony Cassato. Chief of Serenity Police. In his absence, Sheriff Rudder has requested that I act on his behalf."

Brenda was frowning. "Does this autopsy mean you think that someone . . . someone . . . ?"

"No, this is merely routine," Tony replied quietly.

In my ear, Mother whispered, "There's nothing routine about any of this."

142

Tony was saying to Brenda, "But the sheriff and I think an autopsy would be prudent. We think a judge would agree, should you protest. But wouldn't you like to know what caused this?"

"Yes, yes, I would," Brenda said quickly. "If you need my permission, you have it."

"Thank you for cooperating," Tony said.

A filled black body bag was being loaded onto a gurney. Tony went over and spoke to the female paramedic, and they exchanged nods. An ambulance was backing over. Tony helped wave it in while the crowd parted. As interest waned and the process took its time, those who'd been so eager to watch the unfolding drama were getting restless, many returning to other activities.

But no question: the air had gone out of the fete's happy bubble.

Tony came back over and said to the group of board members, "Really, no one should be leaving, but without any officers here, I can't prevent that. So I'll need your help. I need to question everyone who was involved in running the Tombola game. Could you folks round them up for me?"

This took the trustees by surprise, unpleasant surprise in Digby Lancaster's case.

"Is that really necessary?" Digby asked.

Celia began, "Why on earth would —"

"Then," Father Cumberbatch said to Tony, "you *do* consider this a suspicious death."

Tony patted the air with quieting palms. "I need to give Sheriff Rudder a detailed account of exactly what happened here, including the events leading up to Mr. Starkadder's apparent heart attack."

I wondered if the medics had mentioned anything else pertinent to Tony in their hushed conversation with him.

Flora, having dropped her arm from around Brenda, was gesturing to herself with both hands. "Well, there's no need to question *me,* Chief Cassato. *I* wasn't involved in running the game."

Father Cumberbatch cooly put in, "But you *did* help set up the bottles, Flora."

She looked at Tony, her expression sick. "Does that count?"

He nodded. "As I said, I need to talk to anyone involved in staging the game."

"Pardon!"

Tony flinched, as if someone had thrown a punch. He hadn't noticed Mother sidling up next to him.

She said cheerfully, "Don't you think the Community Center would make an excellent place for you to conduct your interrogations . . . that is, interviews?"

144

To his credit, Tony merely drew a single calming breath, which he exhaled before asking her civilly, "And where is that, Vivian?"

The various board members glanced at each other, not sure what to make of Serenity's police chief and their visiting diva being so obviously well acquainted.

But it was Flora who answered, "On Brighton Street — not far."

"What about Fred?" Celia asked. "Where has he gone off to? He should be in on these interviews — he's the one who plucked the tickets out of the drum."

A quick exchange between board members revealed that none of them had seen the handyman since Barclay collapsed.

Father Cumberbatch asked Tony, "Would you like me to try to find him?"

"Please. Then bring him to the center."

The priest departed.

Tony said to Brenda, "I'm afraid I'll need to include you in this. But I promise to keep my questions brief."

She nodded. "That's thoughtful of you, Chief. I . . . I assume I'll need to get to the hospital in Serenity. Won't they be wanting information from me there? Maybe sign some papers?"

"Yes."

Digby asked gruffly, "What about the Tombola raffle? If it's canceled, we'll have to refund the ticket money."

"Callous as it may sound, Chief Cassato," Celia said, stepping forward, "that would really hurt our fund-raising efforts. This is an important day for us."

It did sound callous. But with no town taxes in Old York, I could see why Celia was concerned.

Tony glanced around. The crowd had thinned some, but otherwise the fete was going again, almost full-throttle.

He said, "I see no reason why the raffle can't continue with others running it. But no one who was involved before."

Flora said, "I can find some volunteers from the crowd."

"Okay," Tony said. "Then come to the center."

She ran off. In that latest low-cut thing of hers, she'd have no trouble getting volunteers — male ones, anyway.

Tony followed Celia, Digby, and Brenda across the green toward the Community Center. Mother and I (and Sushi) tagged after. I was a little surprised Tony hadn't told us to stay behind, but maybe he was just too distracted.

Outside the center, Tony got everyone's

name before each of them trooped in. Then he turned to face me.

"Brandy," he said, very quietly, "I could really use your help here."

So that was why we hadn't been banished.

He was saying, in almost a whisper, "I want to keep this somewhat casual. Intimidating these people would be counterproductive. So I won't be taking notes."

"I can record the interviews on my cell. Discreetly, so they don't notice I'm doing it."

"No. Take *notes* on your cell, and send them to me in an e-mail. I don't mean play stenographer and put down the whole interview. Just names, occupations, and . . . highlights. You know what I want. And sit away from us."

I nodded. "Should anyone notice, it'll look like I'm merely texting. People saw us together, so they'll figure I'm just your date. Sitting across the room, bored, waiting for you."

"Perfect."

Mother was taking in all this delicious subterfuge with glittering eyes. "What about me, Chiefie? What sneaky thing can *I* do?"

"You need to do something I would have done already, if my hands hadn't been so full."

"Yes? Yes?"

"Go find that beer bottle."

"It could be the murder weapon!"

"If there's a murder, yes, it could be. Use a hanky or something and bring it here. Do you think you'd recognize it?"

She nodded. "It was rather distinctive. Castle Moat brand. I'll check the trash containers if necessary. No one's selling beer here, after all."

"Right. Now off you go."

Off she went.

"Was that a fool's errand?" I asked him.

"Well, it's an errand and she's a . . . well, we really do need that bottle. And if anyone can find it, it's Vivian Borne."

Inside, I settled on the couch in the front area, Sushi still in her baby carrier. Meanwhile, Celia, Digby, and Brenda found chairs at the large round table. Flora entered, a little out of breath, and behind her came Father Cumberbatch and Fred, who joined the others. Apparently Tony was going to interview them as a group, which seemed wise to me. Individually dealt with, they might feel more like suspects.

I removed Sushi from the sling and tried to settle her on the couch, but she stubbornly jumped down. Trotting across the room to Tony, she pawed at his pant leg, and he smiled and picked Sushi up and began petting her.

Oh that guy of mine was clever. How threatening could a chief of police be if he liked cute little fur balls?

Sushi in his arms, scratching the doggie under her neck, Tony stood before the group. "Thanks for your cooperation. This is just an informal fact-finding exercise."

My thumbs were poised on my cell's keyboard.

Digby said, "You can spare us the soft soap, Chief Cassato. We're here because you figure Barclay Starkadder was murdered."

Brenda stiffened in her chair, her eyes flying to Tony. "Is that right, Chief Cassato?"

Tony, continuing to pet an appreciative Sushi, replied, "At this point, no one is figuring anything. As I said, I need to give Sheriff Rudder a full account of what happened this afternoon."

But every expression at the table seemed skeptical.

Flora had the kind of frown that can precede tears.

"Do we need . . . legal representation?" This began as a question to Tony, but ended up with her going from one face to another at the table.

"You mean," Digby said with a nasty

149

smile, "do we have the right to remain silent? Well, I for one won't be answering *any* questions without my lawyer present."

Tony said, "This is not an official inquiry. I've simply asked you good citizens to help me gather some preliminary information for Sheriff Rudder. Any legal concerns you have can be expressed to him."

My thumbs wrote: **Digby wants a lawyer.**

Father Cumberbatch cleared his throat, and heads turned his way. "I think we, all of us, should cooperate and answer the chief's questions. The sooner we do that, the sooner we can get back to the fete and present a unified front."

"I agree," Celia said, with a nod of finality. "The longer we're here, and not there, the worse it looks."

Brenda turned toward the handyman. "What do you think, Fred?"

Fred shrugged. "I say, sure, let's get this dang thing over with."

Brenda's eyes returned to Tony. "Okay, Chief Cassato, what do you need from me?"

Tony put Sushi down, drew a chair over and sat, but away from the table. "Tell me about your uncle at the fete, Ms. Starkadder, prior to his collapse."

Brenda breathed deep, then let it all out. "Well, Barclay seemed fine at the Tombola

raffle, just his typical, usual, rather . . .
imperious self."

Some sad smiles.

She continued with a thoughtful frown.
"He always got a kick out of the fete. He
was a real Anglophile. So I would say he
was having a good time, just walking
around, nodding to people as if" — she
smiled, laughed lightly — "as if he were doing them a favor."

More sad smiles, even a chuckle or two.

"And," she said, "he was genuinely excited
when he won that bottle of beer . . . maybe
because it was his favorite brand."

She stopped, eyes tearing.

"Take a moment," Tony said gently.

She did, then went on. "As you may have
heard me mention, my uncle said he was
thirsty, and was going to drink the beer then
and there, even after I reminded him it was
against the rules. I knew he'd just taken his
medication, and everyone *knows* it's not a
good idea to —"

"Did the bottle have a twist-off cap?"

"No. A regular one. He had an opener on
his key chain."

"How much of it did your uncle drink?"

"About half, and pretty quickly . . . not
chugging it, but . . . quickly. Then he started
gasping for air — like he couldn't breathe."

Tears were running down her cheeks. "I . . . I felt so *helpless.*"

Flora, seated next to Brenda, handed her a tissue.

"Sorry to put you through this, Ms. Starkadder," Tony said. "Just a few more questions."

"I'm okay," Brenda replied, dabbing at her eyes. "I'm all right. Go on."

"You said the beer was his favorite brand?"

She nodded. "Castle Moat. It's imported."

Flora offered, "The pub carries it."

"What pub is that?"

"The Red Lion, on Cambridge, right next door to my flower shop."

Tony asked the group, "Does anyone know what happened to that bottle? Any of you pick it up, or see someone who did?"

The group exchanged shrugs and raised eyebrows.

Tony pressed. "Does anyone remember seeing the bottle there next to Mr. Starkadder?"

Nobody did.

Brenda said, "Well, it *should* have been there, because I saw it drop from my uncle's hand."

This time it was Tony who shrugged. "The paramedics may have taken it. I'll check."

But they hadn't, or he wouldn't have

pressed the matter here, or sent Mother off searching.

"Thank you, Brenda," Tony said. "I won't keep you any longer. Do you need transportation to the hospital in Serenity?"

"No. We have a car. My uncle and I. But . . . I'm a little shaky. Maybe I shouldn't drive myself."

Fred said to Brenda, "I could drive you over there, Miss Starkadder."

"Would you, Fred? Is that all right, Chief Cassato?"

Tony asked Fred, "You'll be around later? So you'll be available if Sheriff Rudder wants to talk to you?"

"I have to be back for the play tonight. I mean, I assume the show's going on."

Nobody contradicted that, Digby muttering, "We could use the revenue."

"Then go ahead," Tony told them.

In my e-mail I wrote: **Fred Hackney, New Vic Theater, Set Designer/Construction. Withdrew Barclay's winning ticket from drum. Handed it to Digby to announce number.**

Gradually I typed in similar write-ups on everyone being questioned.

Fred was moving away from the table, but Brenda stayed at her seat, though she stood in place there.

She addressed the trustees: "There is something I'd like to say before I leave. Since I'll be taking my uncle's place on the board, you might like to know what my vote on the incorporation issue is. It's the same as his was. . . . *No!* So if someone *did* kill him, and by doing so hoped to change the balance of the board . . . it was for *nothing!*"

Brenda votes no! I typed.

Barclay's niece left the table and marched toward the exit, Fred trailing behind her.

As Brenda neared, I stood from the couch and held out Barclay's jacket, which I'd hung on to. A pained expression crossed her face as she recognized the garment as her uncle's. She took it, held it close, and gave me a grateful nod.

"Say, Fred!" Tony called as they approached the door.

Startled, the handyman stopped and turned. "Yes, sir?"

"Where did you get off to, after Mr. Starkadder collapsed?"

"I went off to fetch those paramedical people, but their tent was empty — they was already on the way over. Seen the fuss over by the Tombola, and just stayed out of the way. Anything else, Chief?"

"No, Fred. That's fine. Just stay available."

154

When the door banged shut after the pair, a flabbergasted Celia cried, "Is that woman accusing one of *us* of killing Barclay?"

"Preposterous," Digby snorted.

"The poor woman's just upset," Father Cumberbatch said. "And she doesn't know what she's saying."

"*Doesn't* she?" Flora asked, an edge in her voice. "Two of the three board members who've been against incorporation are dead, and of those, *I'm* the only one left!"

"Didn't you hear her?" scoffed Digby. "She'll be voting against it, too."

"And Chad's *another* no vote," Celia added. "So it's still three to three."

Flora's chair screeched as she stood and leaned her palms against the table. "Do you people take me for an idiot? I *know* about the clause in the bylaws that allows for emergency meetings."

"So?" Digby said with a shrug.

"So . . . a two-thirds majority of the trustees can call such a meeting *before* Brenda and Chad are installed, and take a vote . . . and guess what?" Flora's upper lip curled back and much of her prettiness evaporated. "Incorporation would pass!"

"Is that true?" Father Cumberbatch asked.

Digby shrugged. "As far as it goes."

The priest arched an eyebrow. "Generally,

155

the truth goes pretty far."

Celia looked up at Flora, who remained standing. "Dear . . . you're getting worked up for nothing. If you think so little of us, then tell me, why didn't we call an emergency meeting after Millie died?"

Flora spat the words: "Because, *dear,* Millie and Barclay and I, *none of us,* would have agreed to an emergency meeting. It would take *two* of us to die for that to happen. And now two have."

The florist's gaze flew to Tony, who had been listening quietly, letting them talk.

"Don't you see, Chief Cassato?" she said. "With just Millie gone, two thirds of five trustees isn't enough for a majority — but with Barclay out of the way . . ."

I gulped — this would require math! — but I took a shot and typed: **2/3 of 5 = 3.3 people needed — one more than yes voters Celia, Digby, Father C. But with Barclay dead 2/3 of the 4 remaining trustees = 2.6 people, and the yes voters could call the emergency meeting and vote for incorporation.**

Digby flew to his feet. "How would you like to be sued for slander?"

"For the love of heaven, Flora," Celia pleaded. "Do you really think that Father Cumberbatch or Digby or I had *anything* to

156

do with Millie's or Barclay's deaths?'"

Flora, suddenly faced with a direct question, stammered, "I . . . I . . . I di-didn't . . . didn't make any direct accusation, but . . . if you were in *my* shoes —"

"That's enough," Tony said. "Flora, Digby, please — sit down."

With embarrassed reluctance, they did.

Tony said, "Nerves are understandably frayed after the loss of Millie and Barclay . . . who both, let's keep in mind, had heart conditions. But making accusations, and threats, is not helpful."

Flora looked sheepish while Digby just sat there glaring, flushed.

"Let's get back to my questions about running the raffle," Tony said, "so we can all get out of here. Maybe even enjoy what's left of the fete."

One at a time, Digby, Father Cumberbatch, and Celia explained their roles in the game. This included what Tony already knew, having been in the crowd: that Fred drew the ticket from the drum and passed it to Digby, who announced the number and then passed it to Father Cumberbatch, who checked the drum ticket against the winner's; and Celia retrieved the corresponding bottle of beer.

But I diligently put all of that down in the

e-mail, anyway.

Finally, Tony asked the group, "Why did it take so many of you to run one game?"

Celia answered, "It's long been a tradition that all the trustees are involved in some aspect of our biggest fete moneymaker."

"I see." His eyes went to Flora. "You mentioned earlier that you'd arranged the bottles on the table before the fete began."

She nodded. "And stuck onto the bottles the labels with numbers that began with five, then ten, fifteen, and so forth, until all the bottles had numbers."

Tony was rubbing his forehead like he had a headache. "I guess I'm not fully understanding."

Celia seemed eager to explain. "Each ticket — with an identical ticket kept by the seller — has two numbers, understand? The larger one at the top — the one Digby called out — is in the thousands, because, well, we could conceivably sell thousands of tickets if the fete drew a large crowd."

"All right," Tony said patiently. "I'm still with you."

She went on. "The smaller number, at the bottom of each ticket, is only in the hundreds because the most bottles we've ever raffled off was about three hundred."

"Okay."

"The numbers I tape on the bottles are in increments of five — beginning with five, then ten, fifteen, and so on, until I run out of bottles."

Tony frowned. "Why not number the bottles one, two, three?"

Impatiently, as if any child would know all this, Digby said, "Because we only put one of every five tickets sold — and you *must* buy five — into the drum. Tickets with numbers ending in a zero or five."

"So," Tony said with a nod, "a person has only a one in five chance of winning."

Celia nodded. "We make more money that way."

"Wouldn't it be simpler," Tony asked, "to charge more money for *one* ticket that has *one* number, and all the tickets go into the drum, and let the winner just pick out his own bottle?"

For a moment no one spoke — they just goggled at him, as if he'd suggested painting a mustache on the *Mona Lisa*.

Then Celia huffed, "Well, that just isn't the Old York way!"

And that was coming from somebody who *wanted* progress!

If people really were being murdered here, I hoped it wasn't over maintaining the Tombola tradition.

Tony, suppressing a smile, said, "Just an outsider's suggestion." He swung his gaze to the florist. "Flora, when you put the bottles on the table, did you arrange them in any particular order?"

She shook her head and red hair bounced and flounced. "No, I just set them up as I pulled them out of the boxes. But the labels? Those I did apply in numerical order . . . otherwise I'd be hunting all over the table trying to find a particular number."

"Fine. How many bottles were there?"

"Let me see . . . the last number on a label was eight hundred and eighty. So, divide that by five . . ." I let her do the math. "One hundred and seventy-six bottles."

"Did a fete committee or you board members or somebody purchase them for the raffle?"

Digby snorted, "Good heavens, no! We'd never make a profit that way."

"They're always donated," Celia said.

"Who by?" Tony asked.

"Some by our local businesses, but mostly Old York citizenry."

"Were any records kept of who gave what?"

"Why should there be?" Digby blurted. "Good God, man, these are decent folks

160

who just want to help raise money for their town."

Tony raised a conciliatory palm. "I'm not implying otherwise. Now, I only have a few more questions before I'm done."

"Well, *I'm* done now," Digby snapped. He pushed back his chair and stood. "Anybody else coming?"

When he saw no one else joining his mutiny, the realtor sailed out.

Tony asked the others, "How was the donation of bottles handled?"

Flora said, "People dropped them off, over a period of several weeks, at any trustee-run establishment — the inn, the theater, the museum, Digby's office, my floral shop. Father Cumberbatch is the only trustee left off the list, since we don't want to turn the church into a liquor store."

"Not *officially* on the list," the priest said with a smile. "But I did have some explaining to do when the bishop paid me a surprise visit and noticed several bottles of whiskey inside the church vestibule."

This brought chuckles from the rest and got a grin out of Tony.

Flora raised her hand as if in class. "Chief Cassato? Something I forgot to mention. This morning, when I was setting up the table, Chad Marlowe delivered the bottles

161

that had been left at the theater. Millie had been scheduled to assist in setting up, so I asked him if he would step in for his grandmother, and help tape on some of the labels. And he did for a while, but then said he had to get back to the theater and left me on my own."

"Did you see Chad after that? At the fete, I mean."

"No."

"Anyone see him at the fete?"

No one had.

Tony nodded, breathed deeply, smiled and said, "That's all the questions I have for now. You'll no doubt be hearing from the sheriff. Thank you for your patience and co-operation."

The group rose from the table all at once and lost little time in getting out of there.

But just as the last of them had gone, Mother came rushing in and up to Tony.

"No sign of the beer bottle," she said, clearly frazzled, tendrils of hair askew. "And believe me, I looked everywhere! My head was in more trash cans than a tomcat looking for supper."

Tony's smile was just slightly sadistic. "Thanks for trying, Vivian."

"Don't you find that suspicious? The missing bottle, I mean?"

"Actually I do. It might mean someone removed it."

"My thinking exactly!"

Tony walked Mother over to join me in the couch area, where I was still sitting next to a curled-up Sushi.

"I've sent you that e-mail," I told him. "I hope you don't take off points for spelling."

His grin was easy. "I promise not to. Thank you."

I said to him glumly, "I suppose you have to go back to Serenity."

He nodded. "Sorry. With Rudder tied up, I need to handle things on that end. We'll have to cut this afternoon short. I was really looking forward to the play."

And I'd been looking forward to talking him into staying over.

"A few things you might find of interest," I said, "that didn't make it into the e-mail."

"Such as?"

I told him that I'd overheard Celia and Father Cumberbatch discussing two large sums of money. And that I'd seen Flora and Digby having an animated conversation.

"Good to know," he said. "But the money could be a reference to renovations for the inn and repairs to the church. And tempers can run high when you're putting on a big event."

"Just trying to help," I said, trying not to sound defensive.

"And I appreciate it. Walk me to my car?"

We did that, Sushi back in her carrier.

Tony stood by the driver's side door of his car, which was parked in front of the inn, and said to Mother, "I hate to miss your performance, Vivian."

"Quite understandable under the circumstances."

He gave me a quick kiss, Sushi a final pat, and got in the car. We watched him back out, wave, and disappear.

"I thought he'd never leave," Mother said. "Now! About that snippet of conversation you heard between Celia and Father Cumberbatch — what were their *exact* words?"

I sighed, thought back. "The priest asked, 'How much?' Then Celia said, 'Twenty thousand each.' "

"Renovations and repairs, my Aunt Olive! Sometimes that boyfriend of yours can be quite obtuse . . . that means thickheaded, dear."

"I know what it means, Mother."

"It seems quite likely there's extortion at play here." She lifted a fingertip to her lips. "And Celia's use of the word *each* might well mean *other* trustees are the target of an extortionist."

"Over what?"

"Their votes, perhaps! And *that* could be what Flora and Digby were arguing about." Her eyes bore in on me. "Experience or witness anything else of interest at the fete, dear?"

"No." I decided not to tell her about Hilda's Cyclops prediction. But then something flashed into my mind. "Mother . . . ?"

"Yes, dear?"

"You gave *your* tickets to Barclay, didn't you?"

"That's right."

"What if the beer in that bottle had been poisoned . . ."

"That's my assumption, yes."

". . . but the bottle was intended for you?"

Mother's eyes went wide. "For *moi*? But why? Whoever would want to see me dead?"

I could have given her a considerable suspect list, but limited myself to this situation. "You've been snooping around, haven't you? And with your reputation for solving murders, somebody may have gotten nervous."

Her eyes were wild as a horse about to throw some poor cowpoke trying to break it. "Yes! Not unlike Poirot showing up on the Orient Express, or a killer learning that Nero Wolfe has been hired to take the case!"

"Let's stick to reality, Mother."

Now she was frowning in thought. "I would know for *sure* who the bottle was intended for, if I had those tickets."

I held up a handful of tickets.

"Heavens to Murgatroyd!" Mother exclaimed. "Wherever did you get *those,* dear?"

"Out of Barclay's jacket pocket, before giving it back to his niece."

Mother took the tickets — nine in all — and arranged them in two groups on the hood of a nearby car.

Pointing to the group of five, she said, "These are *mine,* because I remember folding them — see the crease?"

I did.

She pointed to the group of four. "Those tickets were Barclay's. His winning ticket is missing." She leaned forward, studying the tickets. "That's odd."

"What?"

"The larger numbers on my tickets are higher than the ones on Barclay's."

"So what?"

"*So what,* you ask? Well, dear, the man was *behind* me in the ticket line . . . so his numbers should be higher."

I asked, "The tickets were all on the same roll?"

"Yes, one big roll."

I nodded. "Then, you're right. The numbers should go up as the roll is used, not *down.* Did you notice who the ticket seller was?"

Mother didn't have to think about it. "Fred Hackney."

Fred Hackney, who had drawn Barclay's winning ticket from the drum.

Fred Hackney, who had avoided Tony's questioning by taking Brenda to the hospital.

"Couldn't Fred have started selling the tickets from the other end," I offered, "or maybe used up tickets from last year?"

Frankly, neither explanation seemed very likely to me. But I didn't want Mother so distracted by possible murders that she might give a bad performance tonight.

"Perhaps you're right, dear," Mother said, with a not terribly convincing yawn. "Possibly just being at a fete puts a sort of Agatha Christie cast on things."

"Maybe so, but remember, reality."

"I couldn't agree more." She scooped up the tickets. "I think I'll pop inside for a nap. Why don't we both go in and catch a few relaxing zee's before the big show?"

That sounded like a good idea, and I took her up on it. On the inn's second floor, we exchanged little waves as we retired to our rooms.

But Sushi was giving me a look that said, *You don't really* buy *that, do you?*

A Trash 'n' Treasures Tip

The value of an antique beer bottle is determined by factors such as rarity, age, clarity of the glass, and whether the bottle has an embossed or paper label . . . or if it contains the original beer, which would be extremely rare indeed. It would also be highly sick-making, if you drank it instead of just prized your rare brew.

CHAPTER SEVEN:
PLAY OUT THE PLAY

You are in luck, dear reader, as I, Vivian, have been temporarily handed over the reins of our exciting narrative, which brings to mind a stagecoach pursued by outlaws along a narrow mountain trail, as the driver guides his team of horses with the occasional crack of a whip and no end of colorful exclamations.

But, once again, I must take up valuable space to take issue with some of Brandy's comments; I will limit these corrections to two, as I have been granted only the first half of this chapter (maximum 2,500 word count).

First, Brandy's use of the word *semaphoric* in reference to my acting style is both unkind and inaccurate — *of course* as a stage artiste I often rely upon expressive gesticulation. The theater is not reality but a larger-than-life representation — as a reviewer at the *Quad Cities Reader* once said,

"Vivian Borne's gestures seem designed to help the audience land their collective plane." Precisely my intention! Also, I am aware that the median age of my audiences at the Serenity Playhouse is sixty-five, a time of life when the eyes and ears may begin to falter.

Second, I resent the child's assertion that I am "getting up there." As Nero Wolfe would say, this is sheer flummery! Seventy is the new fifty (not that I admit to being seventy), faltering eyes and ears or not.

After leaving the Horse and Groom Inn — imagine Brandy being so naive as to think I'd need a nap in the midst of a murder inquiry! — I headed straight for the Red Lion Pub. No, Vivian Bourne was not after a stiff drink — rather to drink in info on the stiffs. (Writing students, notice how I cleverly switched that around, although perhaps referring to murder victims as *stiffs* might be viewed as tactless. Art can be cruel!)

The public house (if you were wondering, that's what *pub* is short for) (You're welcome) was on Manchester between Flora's florist shop and a haberdashery. As I entered the Victorian-style building, I had a flash of déjà vu that can't be entirely attributed to my bipolar medication.

The Red Lion was similar to Hunter's in Serenity — that is to say, it was an unlikely combination of bar and hardware store. Apparently, the owners of this establishment also had no problem serving their customers alcohol with a power-tool chaser. (Hunter's now enacted a breathalyzer test for patrons buying certain items, following numerous upon-returning-home accidents, including, but not limited to, nail-gunning a foot to the floor, sawing off a finger, and drilling a hole in a hand. There are more examples, but those — my top faves! — should suffice.)

The claustrophobically low ceiling was typical of a British village pub, as if built in anticipation of a hobbit clientele. To my right was the bar area, with tables and chairs, and a long serving counter whose wall mirror doubled the display of liquor bottles.

To my left was the hardware section, where at the moment a short, stout man with wiry gray hair was busy filling a standee with batteries.

Noticing my entrance, he moved toward me with a smile and an uneven gate. "May I help you, ma'am?"

A name tag pinned near the top of his brown work apron read, "Marty."

"No thank you, Marty," I replied.

"Well, just let me know if I can."

He started away, but I said, "Oh, I do have *one* small question."

He turned and raised a fuzzy white caterpillar of an eyebrow. "Yes?"

"I hope I'm not getting too personal, but I couldn't help noticing your limp. Did you, perchance, lose a leg on a theme-park ride involving a large mechanical mammal with very sharp teeth?"

Marty had the kind of dazed look that I had seen before, from time to time, most often on the face of my psychiatrist at session's end.

"Ma'am," he replied slowly, "I, uh, appreciate your concern . . . I guess . . . but I dropped a paint can on my foot this morning."

"Oh, thank goodness! I thought the coincidence too extreme. But you know, I have a friend, a female, who works in a hardware store back home, who was the victim of such an incident, and I think her infirmity gains her sympathy and sales."

"Is that right."

"So you might consider keeping it in — the limp, I mean. It adds character!"

This dazed look was a new one. The only similar one I'd ever seen was the time (coincidentally) a paint can dropped from the top of my ladder and landed on Brandy's head.

As I headed into the bar area, I could feel the man's eyes following me; it's nice to know, after all these years, that I still have It!

(*Note to Editor:* Please leave *It* capitalized. That's a Clara Bow reference, which will be before your time, but that's what Google is for.) (For the record, before *my* time, too, but I have a professional's sense of history where the acting profession is concerned.)

The tables were empty — not much business during the day's festivities — but one person sat at the counter, a woman in a black sweater and jeans, her back to me.

I sashayed over and hoisted myself up on a stool, politely putting one between us.

"Vivian's the name," I said. "Here for the fete."

She swiveled toward me. A well-preserved forty or perhaps a hard-living thirty, the woman had a once-attractive face betrayed by drink — the hard stuff, judging by what appeared to be a tumbler of whiskey before her.

"Henrietta," she said with a slur. "But everybody calls me Henny."

"Very well, Henny it is."

A stocky female bartender behind the counter asked me, "What can I do you for?"

"A bottle of Castle Moat, please, my dear."

"We've got that on tap, if you'd rather." She had short-cropped brown hair, a plain face void of makeup, and wore a gray sweatshirt with the pub's logo.

I said, "I'd prefer a bottle, if you don't mind."

The bartender shrugged. "Be a minute — it's in the cooler in back."

As she left to get my beer, I twisted to face Henny. "Nice little place here. Locally owned, I assume."

Henny's eyes tried to focus on me. "Yeah, Marty and June. He runs the hardware side, she's behind the bar."

"Are you in town for the fete, dear?"

She shook her head. "Lived here all my life."

"Must be a storybook existence, surrounded by such a delightful ambiance."

"Haul my behind out if I could."

"Well, then, why don't you, dear?"

"Easier said."

June returned with my beer and removed the cap with an opener, some foam brimming up. I am not overly fond of beer, and my medication likes it even less. But one

174

must make sacrifices when pursuing evildo-
ers.

The bottle was halfway to my lips when I
paused to ask, "There doesn't happen to be
a bus due in, leaving for Kalamazoo?"

June smirked and chuckled. "Lady, as a
bartender, I get some unusual questions,
but that's a new one. No, no bus to Kalamazoo due in."

"That's a relief."

June and Henny exchanged glances.

I took a swig from the bottle. Not bad, as
beer went. But it would go no further; I'd
be faking my swigs from now on.

I ventured, "I suppose you've heard about
what happened to Barclay Starkadder?"

My query had been directed to June, but
the response came from Henny — a little
choking sob.

I turned to her. "Oh, I *am* sorry, dear.
Were you and the late Mr. Starkadder
friendly?"

Henny hopped off her stool, spilling her
whiskey a little, then fled to the back, where
a sign directed patrons to the *Kings* and
Queens restrooms.

"Oh, my," I said to June. "I had no intention of upsetting that poor woman."

Wiping up the spill, the bartender replied,
"That's all right — you're not from here.

You'd have no way of knowing."

"Knowing what?"

June ceased mopping. "Henny had a fling with that hound dog, not so long ago."

"Which hound dog would that be?"

"Barclay Starkadder. You can wear fancy threads and still be a hound, you know."

I knew that very well, and not merely from cartoons.

But I said, "Is that right?"

June nodded. "Ol' Barclay dumped her last month, and ever since, she's been a fixture around this place. She always liked a drink, but never like this before."

"What a shame. No man is worth a woman's liver." Well, maybe Clark Gable.

"Worst of it is," the bartender was saying, "Henny left her happy home for that Brylcreemed bum, and now her hubby's filed for divorce, and the kids are going with him."

"Poor darling."

"You ask me? Getting dead? Couldn't happen to a nicer guy."

I took a pseudo sip. "I'm sure you don't mean that, June."

"Oh don't I? Henny's only the latest in a long line of gals that man has loved and left — some of them pretty darn prominent in our little village."

I was leaning forward. We were coconspirators now. "Such as . . . ?"

She leaned in to whisper. "Such as . . . well, let's just say one of our trustees."

My surprise was genuine. "You don't say! You wouldn't be talking about Celia Falwell, by any chance. You see, I'm staying at the inn, and I've, uh, seen her husband."

June shook her head. "I mean that redheaded flirt — Flora Payton."

"Oh, I think she's rather sweet. Bought some flowers from her for my room. Attractive lady."

"She's a dish, all right, and nice enough as far as it goes. But she sure does like to prance around with her blossoms showing."

Another fake sip. "Barclay and the florist — ended badly, did it?"

"I'll say! Flora threatened to *kill* Barclay in this very establishment, the night he broke it to her that he was throwing her over for Henny." She grunted a humorless laugh. "He must have known she'd react badly, and that's why the coward picked a public place — only it backfired on him."

"How did Flora feel about her replacement?"

"Henny? Well, naturally, Flora was upset with her at the time. But after Barclay dumped Henny? Those two gals became

177

sisters in arms in the We Hate Barclay Starkadder Society."

Apparently not an exclusive club.

I nodded toward the restroom, where Henny was still holed up. "Apparently your friend hasn't gotten over Barclay."

June rolled her eyes. "Henny was at the fete when he fell over and died. Saw the whole deal from a ringside seat."

"At the Tombola game, you mean?"

She nodded. "Henny came in here right after it happened and told me all about it . . . and climbed into a bottle."

A group of boisterous men entered the bar and took up residence at several tables. With no alcohol served at the fete, this was bound to happen.

I managed one final question. "Can you re-cap my bottle, dear? I'd like to take it with me."

"Sure. No problem."

From beneath the counter, June got a gizmo that looked something like a wine cork remover with handles. She took my bent cap and put it in the gizmo, then placed the gizmo on top of my bottle and forced the handles down.

June handed me the Castle Moat. "Good as new."

I examined the cap. "It really is. Looks

like it's never been opened. Is that tool hard to come by?"

"Heck no. Marty sells 'em in the hardware section. Some people like to make their own brew, y'know. Excuse me, ma'am, I got customers to tend to."

I thanked her, slid off my stool, and my beer bottle and I left the pub-cum-hardware store. Across the way on the village green the festivities were still in full sway, if somewhat subdued in the aftermath of Barclay's abrupt departure.

Continuing along Manchester Street, I passed Flora's Floral Shoppe, closed for the fete, then turned right onto London Street. I was drooping a little by the time I'd reached the inn — still time for that nap I should be taking on this afternoon before a performance — when I froze in my tracks, any drowsiness instantly disappearing.

The outside sign carried a new message. ONE LAST NO TO DIE.

Brandy back at the helm, assuring you that no extended metaphor about ships and sailing will be inflicted upon you. In my room, I was happily asleep when Mother nudged me unhappily awake.

"Brandy dear! It's time to rise and shine, and I do mean shine, in the best theatrical sense. Time to get up and get ready for tonight's performance, sweets!"

I yawned, got out of bed — Sushi only burrowing farther beneath the covers — and headed into the tiny broom closet of a shower. And this represented Old York's idea of progress.

Twenty minutes later, I was coiffed and dressed in my "theatrical assistant" togs — a black Kamali Kulture Lycra dress and matching flats — to make me unobtrusive as I stood in the wings handing Mother her different hats. (If I had to take part in a theatrical performance, let me do so in a role that truly did fade away.) Also, I had a small, black Coach cross-body bag for a few things like my cell, room key, and some cash.

Mother was already in costume, a purple choir robe that passed for the various characters, the hats alone indicating each identity. (She had "borrowed" the robe from the music room at our church, New Hope.)

(*Mother to Brandy:* Your implication that I stole that robe is completely out of line. I borrowed it, no quotation marks needed, with full intention of returning it as soon as we got back.)

(*Brandy to Mother:* Then I expect you left a note for the choir director, telling him as

180

much. Because if you didn't, then you "borrowed" it.)

(*Mother to Brandy:* As it happens, I didn't leave a note. Simply not necessary. There were extra robes and it wouldn't be missed.)

(*Editor to Vivian and Brandy:* Ladies?)

(*Vivian to Editor:* Apologies.)

(*Brandy to Editor:* Sorry.)

With Sushi left behind in my room, Mother and I departed the inn, where we found Seabert out front picking up that irksome sign.

Seeing us, he grumbled, "I don't know who's been leaving these sick messages, but since it won't stop, Celia's having me remove the sign."

"A wise decision, in the absence of security cameras," Mother said. "Horses on the moon are one thing . . . threats a different matter."

Especially when it seems someone might be carrying them out. The threats I mean, not the horses.

I said, "Why not set a trap?"

Seabert snapped, "I have no intention of hiding in the bushes."

I might have been willing to, if he'd provided a good supply of Twizzlers (strawberry). But that didn't seem likely from such a grouch, so I kept that idea to myself.

Anyway, there was a show to put on.

The innkeeper was hoisting the board on its metal stand to haul it inside as Mother and I turned in the direction of Stratford-on-Avon and the theater.

On the village green, the fete had finally come to a close, volunteers dismantling the tents and picking up debris. In the aftermath of a great social event, there's often an air of deathlike melancholy, and that was especially so in this instance.

On the short walk to the New Vic, Mother — purple robe flapping in the cool breeze — admitted she hadn't gone back to the inn for a nap ("No! Really?") but had instead gone to the Red Lion Pub. She reported encountering one of Barclay's discarded lovers and told me how easy it was to recap a beer bottle.

As we approached the theater, Mother said, "Things are getting very intriguing, dear. I need to question Fred about why the numbers on my tickets were higher than Barclay's when the man was *behind* me in line."

I took her arm, halting her. "Fine, but do that *after* the play, Mother, okay? We don't need the distraction right now. Rehearsal didn't go just . . . tickety boo, remember? More like floppity boom."

"Point well taken, dear. I will table my investigation until after this evening's performance. An actor must leave his or her personal life at the stage doors! As a great thespian once said, 'All is make-believe within those precious walls.' "

"Right. What great thespian?"

"Vivian Borne, dear, Vivian Borne."

I had to ask.

We entered the lobby where black-haired, black-garbed, multipierced Glenda was within her box-office booth getting ready for customers. She nodded to us, then gave us a muffled, "Good luck!"

This threw Mother, and she didn't have to tell me why. "Break a leg" was the only proper well-wishing allowed inside these "precious walls." But Morticia Von Munster apparently didn't know that.

Chad came out of the office to greet us as we passed on our way backstage. Like Glenda, he was in black, though there was nothing Goth about it — a retro tight suit with narrow lapels, white shirt, narrow black tie. The normally blasé young man seemed unusually nervous. But then, he was in charge tonight, not his grandmother.

"I don't know if we'll have much of an audience," he said, in an odd mix of apology and accusation. "Not after these damn deaths."

Mother frowned. "Your grandmother informed me that over one hundred tickets had been presold."

Chad shrugged. "That doesn't mean they'll come. Presolds are often merely a donation, you know, a show of support. Just thought I should warn you it might be a light house."

Mother thrust out her chin as if begging for a punch. "No matter, my dear. Vivian Borne never stints on a performance, whether she plays to twenty or two thousand!"

(Or three, for her one-woman show of Libby Wolfson's *I'm Taking My Own Head, Screwing It on Right, and No Guy's Gonna Tell Me It Ain't.* Two, after intermission.)

I said, "I assume all of the trustees will be here."

"The living ones, anyway," Chad said with a humorless smirk. "And Brenda mentioned she's coming with Father Cumberbatch."

Mother asked, "Will the good father be giving a benediction before the performance?"

"Yes," Chad said. "But for *two* people, now."

"I do hope he'll keep it brief. Could cast a pall on the evening."

184

Not to mention cut into her performance time.

Mother asked, "I hope Fred has made it back from Serenity."

"He has," Chad said. "You'll find him backstage."

We indeed found the handyman in the wings, positioning the card table I used for the hats.

Somehow Mother managed to keep her word about not questioning Fred about the tickets. But she did ask, "How's Brenda coping?"

Fred, in a navy broadcloth shirt and chino slacks, replied, "She's doin' all right, Mrs. Borne. She's even comin' tonight."

"Chad said as much," Mother replied. "Quite commendable, even brave, considering what she's been through. Perhaps a little harmless diversion will keep her mind off all this unpleasantness."

Since the Scottish play was such a light, fun confection.

Fred was nodding. "And she especially wants to be here tonight, 'cause her uncle's favorite Shakespeare play was *Macbeth.*"

Mother cringed at the word and looked up as if the ceiling, or perhaps the sky above it, might fall. *We are in for it now,* her expression said. As for me, I didn't need anybody to mention *Macbeth* out loud to feel that doom was almost upon us.

The handyman was saying, "Anyway, Barclay was lookin' forward to seeing just how you were going to condense the play."

Mother's eyes now went to the card table nearby. "Fred dear, with apologies for this sudden change of staging, I want to try something different tonight."

"Wait, what?" I blurted, alarmed. "I don't think making *any* new changes is a good idea this late in the game."

Deaf to my words, Mother instructed Fred, "I'd like that table *onstage* instead of in the wings."

"What?" I protested. "You mean *my* table? My table of hats?"

Her expression was kindly, but her eyes were Jack the Ripper's. "Dear, it's a burden for me to have to cross the boards to a wing, in order for you to hand me each hat. It puts my timing completely off. *That* is what was wrong at dress."

"What about *my* timing?"

As we discussed this, Fred was already moving the table out onto the stage. "Where ya want it, Mrs. Borne?"

"Left of center, yes . . . a little more — *stop!* Perfection. *Thank* you, Frederick."

My head couldn't have been spinning

more if I'd been leaning over the top of the Empire State Building looking down. "So, what then? I'm . . . I'm supposed to stand next to the table?"

"Dear, I wouldn't think you'd want to be *seen.*"

"Well, *of course* I don't want to be seen!"

"Quite right, dear. So. We'll have you sit *under* the table — you and the hats."

Darn that Fred for saying *Macbeth* out loud! Already the Scottish play was bringing down its curse. . . .

"Now, Fred," Mother said, "can you find a black cloth to cover the table so Brandy can't be seen? And of course she'll need a flashlight."

"No problem," he replied, and went off to get the two items.

Now I felt like I was *falling* from over the side of the Empire State Building. Somehow I managed to face Mother. "You want to change the staging *an hour out*? That's not just a bad idea, it's a *really* bad idea. And I won't do it! Not under any circumstances! I won't, I won't, I *won't!*"

So I'm under the table with the hats and a flashlight, to help me see what I'm doing. I sit cross-legged, and one foot is already asleep. The curtain is already up because Mother wants the audience to get used to the sparse stage.

Through a little hole in the drop cloth, I can see people filing in to the auditorium. I watch as the trustees enter in a group — Celia, Digby, Flora, and Father Cumberbatch with Brenda — but they part company and find various aisle seats (helpful for bathroom breaks and bailing on terrible performances).

It's a respectable turnout after all, and five minutes out, Chad closes the auditorium doors, then sits in the otherwise empty back row.

Father Cumberbatch rises from his aisle seat, walks purposely to the stage steps, and ascends.

The auditorium hushes as he moves to the center of the apron, pauses, then speaks in a reverent voice. "Let's begin the evening with a silent prayer for Millicent Marlowe and Barclay Starkadder, two of Old York's most valued citizens, taken from us prematurely. Please bow your heads."

Most folks do. But some don't, including Digby Lancaster.

After a seemingly endless minute of silence, the priest begins the Lord's Prayer, and the audience joins in. Even Digby. Even a theatrical assistant in black under a cloth-draped card table.

Afterward, Cumberbatch gives a five-minute eulogy — during which time Mother fidgets in the wing, clearly irritated by this upstaging — then the priest returns to his seat.

The lighting technician drops the auditorium into darkness. A spotlight shines center stage, into which a purple-robed Mother strides, wearing a witch's hat.

" 'When shall we three meet again?' " the first witch cackles loudly.

Mother hops to a different spot. " 'When the hurly-burly's done,' " says the second witch.

Again, Mother jumps to a new position. " 'That will be ere the set of sun,' " cackles the third witch. And my flashlight goes out.

Thank you, Fred, you spouting-Macbeth-*out-loud-jerk!*

I feel around in the dark for the hats needed in the next scene, which is between Macbeth and Banquo, captains on the battlefield. Mother's feet appear in back of the table, her hands come down, reaching under the tablecloth, and I fill them with two hats.

She steps back into the spotlight.

" 'So foul and fair a day I have not seen,' " cries Macbeth (only Mother is wearing Lady Macbeth's lacy bonnet).

The audience titters.

Mother changes positions and hats.

" 'How far is't call'd to Forres?' " asks Banquo in King Duncan's crown.

The audience laughs.

Mother's feet return.

I lift the cloth. "Take a bow and quit, Mother."

She leans down, indignant.

"What?" she whispers. "Did Sarah Bernhardt ever quit? Or Lillie Langtry? Never! Give me a hat."

I do.

" 'O, never shall sun that morrow see!' " cries Lady Macbeth, wearing her husband's helmet.

The audience howls.

In for a penny . . .

Mother accelerates, speaking her lines faster, hopping around quicker, like she's in a Keystone Kops silent.

I'm not proud of what happens next. I shove all the hats out onto the stage, like going "all in" in poker, then — lifting the table up on my back, carrying it with me — duck-walk quickly toward the wings, a table with six legs attempting an exit.

But the helmet-wearing Lady Macbeth notices my would-be escape. "Oh, no you don't!"

190

Not a line from Shakespeare, much less the Scottish play, but the audience reacts with peals of laughter.

Mother grabs the tablecloth, thrusts it off magicianlike, exposing me beneath. Gasps of laughter rock the house as she pulls the table off me, while I keep on duck-walking to the wing, lacking only Chuck Berry's guitar, as the crowd screams with laughter.

As Mother valiantly carries on, I hide in a dressing room. But, later, when I hear thunderous applause, I come out and stand in the wing, watching Mother take bow after bow.

What the . . . ?

She sees me and motions for me to join her, and I do, and we bow together, as if the play had come off exactly as intended. Better, even.

Afterward, Celia was the first to come up onstage to congratulate us.

"You both were *marvelous,*" the innkeeper beamed. "Millie had kept it *completely* secret!"

Mother asked, "Kept what secret, dear?"

"That you planned to present the play as such a broad comedy!"

Not missing a beat, Mother said, "Perhaps Millicent wanted to keep that as a surprise."

The other trustees surrounded us.

191

"I don't think this delightful farce could have come at a better time for Old York," Father Cumberbatch said, chuckling all the way. "If ever a performance lifted a community's spirts, *this* is it."

Flora, wiping beneath her eyes with a tissue, laughed. "You quite destroyed my mascara!"

When Digby didn't voice his opinion, Mother asked, "And how did you like our unique Shakespearean interpretation, Mr. Lancaster?"

"Seen worse," he said, grudgingly.

Flora elbowed him. "Come on, Digby! Give it up for the girls. I saw you laughing your head off."

He smiled, maybe for the first time in his life. "Okay. That *was* pretty funny."

Finally Brenda joined our little group.

"I really enjoyed the play," she graciously told Mother and me.

"Thank you, dear," Mother said. "Very sweet of you to say. What part did you like the best?"

"Oh . . . simply all of it. And I'm *sure* my uncle would have loved it, too."

I doubted that.

"Vivian and Brandy," Celia said, "we're having a little after-party at the Red Lion . . . would you lovely ladies, our *stars*, please join us?"

I could have gone for a drink about then, but the decision was Mother's, and she demurred. "Thank you, but it's been a long day. And we need to see Fred about some theater business. Where *is* our trusty stage-hand, by the way?"

"Oh," Father Cumberbatch said, "he's over at the church."

Mother frowned. "Is that right?"

"Yes. He said he wouldn't be needed at the theater, and was going to leave just after the play got going, so he could finish up the ceiling repairs before tomorrow's service."

"Well, he really shouldn't have left his post here," La Diva Borne said, miffed. "What if something hadn't gone as planned?"

"No harm, no foul, Mother," I said.

The father said, "I'm heading over to the church now. We could walk together . . . ?"

"You're not coming to the party, Father?" a disappointed Flora asked.

"Sorry, no, Miss Payton. I have my sermon to go over. And, under the circumstances, I don't really think it would be appropriate."

Chad appeared on the periphery and called, "Nice job, Vivian and Brandy." The compliment came quick and perfunctory. His eyes moved off us. "Brenda? Could I speak to you a moment? In the office?"

"Sure," she said with a smile.

As Chad and Brenda broke away, I began gathering up the hats scattered about the stage, and took them to a dressing room for temporary storage. I had no doubt Mother would be going over to the church.

By the time I got back to the stage, only Mother and Father Cumberbatch remained.

"Ah, there you are, dear," Mother said. "Shall we go see how our absent stagehand is doing?"

We left the now-deserted auditorium, and were crossing the lobby when Brenda came out of the office, her expression dour.

"Brenda," Father Cumberbatch asked, "is something wrong?"

"No, no. It's nothing." She forced a smile. "I'm fine, really. It's just been . . . well, it's been a *day*, hasn't it?"

"Yes, it has," Mother said. "Can we walk you home, dear? I assume you're not up for going to the after-party."

"You assume right. Tonight, I think I just want to be alone."

"Yes," Mother said. "There are times when Garbo really had it right."

Brenda clearly didn't know what Mother was talking about, but she didn't ask for clarification. We started out in the same direction, along Stratford-on-Avon toward

Canterbury Lane.

"Really, there *is* something wrong," Brenda said suddenly.

We all paused, half circling around her.

Very troubled, she said, "Chad just told me that my uncle had been loaning the theater some of our antique swords for their productions."

Mother babbled, "How thoughtful of your uncle! There's nothing quite like the clang of real metal during the sword fight between Hamlet and Laertes in act five, scene two."

"Mrs. Borne, you don't understand," Brenda said. "Uncle Barclay didn't have the authority to loan *any* museum piece to *anybody* — his contract specifies that. And, well, now I have to *wonder. . . .*"

"You have to wonder," Father Cumberbatch said gently, "what *other* authority he may have exceeded?"

She nodded.

"Brenda," the priest said, his voice soothing, "I'm sure this was just a singular lapse in judgment."

"Anyway," I said, "you'll be getting the swords back, won't you?"

"Yes, tomorrow. I'm to call Chad at the theater."

"Well then, no worries, my dear," Mother said cheerfully. "And *you'll* be in charge of the museum now, or soon will be, after your appointment by the trustees."

"I imagine you're right. And let me tell you, the first thing I'm going to do is take a *complete* inventory."

With Brenda's spirits lifted, we pressed on, parting ways with the woman at Canterbury Lane.

Despite the half-moon, the night was dark, and a (working) flashlight would have come in handy, walking down Canterbury Lane toward the church — even without a murderer afoot.

I was glad the priest was with us, otherwise Mother most certainly would have brought up my inexcusable stage behavior. As it was, they discussed the differences between Anglo-Saxon and Norman architecture, while I lagged behind, the grassy path not wide enough for three abreast.

Soon the Gothic church was silhouetted against the night sky, lights from the sanctuary becoming a beacon.

Father Cumberbatch used a key to unlock the heavy wooden door, then pushed it open, its hinges squeaking in protest. We stepped into the dark vestibule and our heavenly host (so to speak) moved to a wall switch to turn on an overhead light.

We moved through the nave and into the

mouth of the sanctuary, where at the far end, in front of the altar, a high scaffolding rose to the domed ceiling.

But Fred was not up there on the platform.

We were following Father Cumberbatch down the center aisle when he stopped so abruptly that Mother ran into him.

"What is it?" she asked.

The priest turned an ashen face toward us. His mouth was moving, but no sound came out.

Then I saw what he had: the twisted body of Fred Hackney, at the base of the scaffolding, like a religious statue that had taken a bad tumble.

A really bad tumble.

A TRASH 'N' TREASURES TIP

When the purchase of an early period antique — say a Louis XIV armchair — is cost-prohibitive, consider buying a good replica, which can be aesthetically pleasing and still have some resale value. And if you sit on it and it breaks, you won't have to be there on your behind, crying, in the ruins. (Ask Mother, but don't mention my name.)

CHAPTER EIGHT:
WHAT'S DONE IS DONE

When Father Cumberbatch began to rush forward, toward the fallen handyman at the base of the scaffolding, Mother grabbed the priest by the arm and held him back firmly. We were poised three-quarters of the way down the center aisle of the sanctuary.

"I'm afraid, Father," Mother said solemnly, "the last rites will have to wait."

He pulled out of her grasp, with unpriestly irritation. "Fred might still be alive!"

"I assure you he's not. It's obvious the poor man's neck is broken."

And even from here, that was indeed obvious. No one could be alive with his head, his neck, twisted in that ungodly position.

A rush of air came from the priest, as if he'd been punched in the stomach. "You sound quite sure of yourself, Mrs. Borne."

"I *have* had some experience," Mother said, with a tinge of tasteless pride. "I also know not to disturb a crime scene."

That startled Cumberbatch and he blinked at us. "Is *that* what this is? Surely this is a tragic accident — Fred up on the platform, losing his footing. . . ."

"Possibly," Mother replied. "But we all know that Fred Hackney was an experienced workman . . . and that this tragedy comes in the wake of two other suspicious deaths here in Old York."

Shaken, the priest swallowed and nodded. He was blister pale.

"Let's look at this calmly," Mother said. "Start at the beginning. You had to unlock the front door."

Cumberbatch nodded. "I asked Fred to keep things locked up here whenever he was working alone. There was some pilfering a while ago, nothing major, but still. . . ." His eyes kept returning to the body.

"Keep your attention right here, Father, on me. Now. Fred had his own key?"

"He did."

"Anyone else have one?"

"Besides myself and Fred? No one. No one at all."

"Is there another way in?"

The priest nodded toward the altar. "There's an emergency exit door back there, but it's a push-bar and doesn't have a key."

"Can it be opened from the outside?"

"No. As I said, it's an emergency exit."

"How about the windows? Do you keep them locked?"

"Yes, those that can be opened at all."

"Very good," Mother said with a nod. "Now, I think it's time for you to call Sheriff Rudder and inform him of poor Mr. Hackney's demise."

Mother delegating this duty surprised me — I knew all too well how much she relished making 911 calls.

Cumberbatch hesitated, his eyes moving fast, hysteria trying to assert itself and falling just short. "But what should I *say* to him? How do I describe what happened? *Was* this an accident or not?"

"That's for the sheriff to determine, Father," Mother said. "Now — the call?"

She might have handed him her cell phone, since Rudder was on speed-dial, but she didn't. Was she up to something?

"Yes, of course," the priest said. "I'll use the office phone."

Mother waited until the priest had gone, then sprang into action, moving briskly down to Fred's body.

I cleared my throat in an *ah-hem* manner. "Mother dear, what was that about not disturbing a crime scene?"

"I'm not *disturbing* it, dear — I'm examining it. There's a considerable difference."

She crouched over the corpse, knees popping, as if a monkey were cracking its knuckles.

Fred, in a typically paint-splattered T-shirt and jeans, lay sprawled on his back on the stone floor, legs bent impossibly, arms outstretched, head twisted unnaturally to one side, eyes open in a face frozen in surprise.

Mother searched the front pockets of his jeans, found a key like the one the priest had used to let us in, examined it in her palm, then returned it to the pocket.

"Darling girl!" Mother called. "Your assistance is needed." She was holding out a hand.

She couldn't get up by herself, and I helped her to her feet. But she still had to brace herself on the scaffolding.

"Well?" I asked. "What's your take on this?"

"I'm not sure, dear. Have you an opinion?"

Asking me meant she was really reaching.

I said, "Coincidence or not, this just about *had* to be an accident. The front door was locked, Fred had the only extra key. No one can get in through the back. Windows are locked."

Mother raised a declamatory finger. "Ah! But our late handyman could have let someone in on some pretext — a friend, a business acquaintance."

"If it was business, he would have conducted that business near the door, after letting them in."

She shook her head, once. "But if it was a protracted conversation, Fred might well have gone back to work and whoever-he-let-in could have followed him to the scaffolding and . . ."

When she trailed off, I said, "And what? Faked an accident, and gone back out, and . . ."

My turn to trail off.

The key had been in Fred's pocket.

"What we have here," Mother said, "is a locked room mystery."

"No we don't. Just because you consider yourself a great detective doesn't make every situation a mystery and every accident a murder. Fred was tired and frazzled from a long, difficult day. Couldn't he just have fallen off that scaffolding?"

"I suppose." Mother lowered her voice. "Does it strike you as suspiciously convenient that Father Cumberbatch offered to accompany us here to the church, *after* we

202

mentioned it was our intention to see Fred?"

"You mean, might he have used us as an alibi?" I shook my head. "He has the only other key . . ."

"My point exactly."

". . . but in any case, I just can't see that man as a killer. Now, as for some of the *other* trustees —"

I shut my trap because the priest was coming down the center aisle.

"Sheriff Rudder is on his way," he told us.

"How long before his arrival?" Mother asked.

Cumberbatch shrugged. "He was about forty minutes away. Soon."

"Well," she replied, almost cheerfully, "I'm sure you can give him a full report when he arrives."

Cumberbatch, taken aback, asked, "You're not *leaving*?"

Mother shrugged. "There's no reason for us all to stay here twiddling our thumbs. Your church, your responsibility."

The priest blanched at her insensitivity. "Well, the sheriff will want to talk to you and your daughter, surely."

"You may inform Sheriff Rudder that we'll make ourselves readily available for any questions — he has my cell number." She raised a cautionary finger. "But I strongly

203

urge you to stay off your cell phone and not tell *anyone* about Mr. Hackney's death until Sheriff Rudder gives his blessing. Otherwise, you could have the entire grounds and church itself overrun with gawkers. Understood?"

Cumberbatch nodded. "Understood."

"Splendid." Then, as if summoning a pup, she said, "Come, Brandy."

And I followed Mother out.

Outside on the stoop in the cool night air, I asked, "Why the quick exit?"

She never left a possible crime scene voluntarily.

Her eyes were dancing with excitement. "Dear, a unique opportunity to identify the killer has presented itself."

"And what would that be?" Assuming there *was* a killer.

Her hands hugged each other. "Don't you think the stars of tonight's acclaimed performance owe the after-party a drop by? Allowing us the chance to join the trustees in the festivities before Fred Hackney's passing is common knowledge?"

No wonder she'd told the priest not to tell anybody but the sheriff about the tragedy.

She was saying, "Of course *we* won't mention Fred's death."

I grinned, getting it. "Giving us the opportunity to see if that unnerves anyone."

"Exactly, dear. All of the board knew that we were heading over to the church. The killer's head will be spinning, wondering what on earth is happening."

We began walking along the darkened lane.

"One of trustees," Mother was saying, "could have sneaked out of the theater during our performance, gone to the church, got let in by Fred, pretended to leave, then, after Fred went back to work on the ceiling —"

"Climbed the scaffolding and pushed him off? Is that even possible?"

"It's not that difficult to climb a scaffolding, dear. Before my double-hip replacement, I could have scampered up there like a monkey."

An image of a monkey with her face doing just that popped into my head. How I wished it hadn't.

Mother dramatically wiped the night sky with a hand. "And there was poor Fred, up on the platform, painting the ceiling, his back to the killer, when that person unknown gave him a shove over the side."

A monkey with her face. And a double-hip replacement. Cracking its knuckles.

"Mother, that still doesn't solve the key

problem — that is, the problem of the key."

She shrugged. "Perhaps there's another key after all. Duplicates can be made easily enough."

"Okay, but why kill Fred? He's not a trustee. His death doesn't have any impact on the incorporation issue."

"Then he must have known too much! He must have seen something!"

We had reached the corner of Cambridge and London.

Mother asked, "Did you happen to notice where the trustees were sitting in the audience?"

"I didn't happen to notice," I said. "I made a point of it. They all had aisle seats, not grouped together in any way. But after the house lights went down, I couldn't see them."

"So one of them could have slipped out during the performance, killed Fred, and come back."

"I guess that's possible."

We were cutting diagonally across the green to Manchester Street.

"But again," I asked, "why *Fred*? And don't say he knew too much."

She gestured with an open hand. "Perhaps he was involved in Barclay's death. Or Millie's."

"An accomplice, you mean?"

"Precisely. The accomplice of someone who decided to tie off a loose end."

We had arrived at the Red Lion. We went in, Mother having already clued me in about the pub/hardware store's similarity to Hunter's back in Serenity, but that didn't make it any less strange. At least the hardware section was closed, and dark, a metal fence separating bar patrons from hammers and chain saws and the like. Probably a good thing.

The pub was crowded, though not unpleasantly so, and the absence of the usual barroom thumping, mind-numbing music was a relief, with only a low-volume selection of British Invasion tunes from the sixties to provide ambiance. We wove our way through the chattering, laughing patrons to the counter, Gerry of the Pacemakers lightly singing, "How Do You Do It?" as we found a spot to stand between taken-up stools.

Bartender June, somewhat frazzled but clearly pleased with the brisk business, currently was occupied filling a tray of glasses with draw beer. While we waited to get her attention, Flora floated over.

"Oh, you're here after all!" She had to raise her voice over the din and the Pacemakers. "Come join us!"

We followed the florist to a corner table for six, where Digby and Celia sat next to each other, their backs to the wall. Flora sat next to Celia, while Mother and I took chairs across from the trio.

Digby asked us, "Fred coming?" He had a mixed drink in front of him.

"Afraid he can't make it," Mother answered.

From our position we were able to unobtrusively watch the triumvirate closely, well placed to pick up on a facial tic or eye twitch or anything else that might give the culprit away.

Celia asked, "Still working on the church ceiling, then? Hard worker, our Fred." She had a martini with extra olives.

"No," Mother replied, "I think he was finished."

Not a twitch. Not a tic.

Flora asked, "Too tired to join us?" She had a glass of red wine.

Following Mother's lead, I said, "Maybe. He was lying down on the job when we got there."

Nothing.

"Good for him," Celia said. "He's going to work himself to death if he isn't careful."

Who was playing word games with who? Whom?

Celia was saying, "Between the theater, and church, and now the museum, ol' Fred doesn't have any social life at all. No wonder he's still single."

Digby frowned. "What's this about work he's doing at the museum?"

Celia shrugged. "Oh, I don't know exactly, just some handyman stuff Brenda has him doing, I guess."

"What *kind* of work?" Digby persisted.

What was his problem?

Frowning, Celia almost snapped at him as she said, "I told you, Digby, I have no idea. I only mention it because I saw Fred carting some tools into the museum — It's not my turn to look after him!"

"Well, it should be somebody's!"

Flora said, "What are you talking about, Digby?"

The realtor frowned. "The village owns the museum, and the board didn't authorize any repairs or renovations. *We're* who Hackney will be sending his bill to."

Celia sighed. "Money, that's all you ever talk about. If you're so worried about it, take it up with Brenda."

"I would if she were here," he grumbled. "I certainly can't take it up with her uncle. . . ."

"Wait," Flora said, "she *is* here. What do

you know, she just walked in!" The florist half stood, waving to get Brenda's attention.

Mother and I twisted around to see Brenda pushing frantically through the crowd, on her way over.

At the table, she stood between Mother and me and said, "What is this, eat, drink, and be merry? Don't you know that Fred is dead?"

Mother and I, exchanging glances, knew that our ability to sit back while somebody incriminated him- or herself had been severely curtailed by this premature announcement.

Had Father Cumberbatch blabbed?

The three board members, uniformly startled, blurted words of disbelief.

Brenda asked them, "You didn't *know* he fell off his scaffolding? He broke his neck."

"We didn't," Celia said, speaking for the others.

Brenda gestured to Mother and me. "You mean, *they* didn't tell you? They were the ones who *found* him — these two and Father Cumberbatch."

Accusatory eyes were on us.

"Over to you," I whispered to Mother.

She cleared her throat. "Brenda is quite right. Sorry to say, Fred Hackney no longer

210

dwells among the living."

I groaned inwardly.

Celia's upper lip curled back. "So — when you came in here, you *knew*? And didn't *say* anything?"

"Why spoil your evening?" Mother asked innocently.

"But we *asked* you about Fred," Flora said. "You *lied* to us."

Mother tilted her head, narrowed her eyes, and raised a qualifying finger. "Lied? Not really. If you think back to my exact *words* —"

"Never *mind* your exact words, Mrs. Borne," Digby growled. "You certainly misled us. One might even think you were trying to slip one of us up. In your muddled mind, I suppose we're all suspects."

I jumped in. "First of all, it's an apparent accident, so nobody suspects anybody." I couldn't look at Mother while I said that. "Second, we didn't think we should tell anyone what happened till Sheriff Rudder arrived . . . and we left before he got there." I craned to look up at Brenda, who remained standing. "How did *you* find out, Ms. Starkadder?"

"Well, I went to the church —"

Mother interrupted: "Dear, do please sit

211

down. My neck is hurting. Eyes at a level, please."

Brenda sank into the chair next to Mother. "I went to the church to ask Fred why he hadn't told me about my uncle loaning the theater those antique swords."

Mother began a cheerful interrogation. "Why go to Fred about it, dear?"

"Well, he was in charge of props."

"Ah. Of course."

"Anyway, when I got there, Father Cumberbatch wouldn't let me in at first, but finally I got him to open up and tell me what was going on." She paused. "Then the sheriff pulled up, lights flashing, and told me to leave."

Mother asked, "Did the sheriff mention wanting to see me, by any chance?"

"No."

Mother seemed hurt, though she should have been relieved.

Brenda continued: "And the sheriff didn't say *not* to tell anyone, so I thought you board members had a right to know." She shook her head slowly. "In a way, it's my fault."

Mother asked, "Why is that, dear?"

"If Fred hadn't taken me to the hospital in Serenity, to deal with what happened to my uncle, he would have finished the church ceiling this afternoon, not tonight. He prob-ably felt rushed and was tired and . . . oh, this is just awful."

Mother patted the woman's arm. "There, there, dear, you couldn't know what would happen. Brandy, get Brenda some water — or would you prefer something stronger?"

"No, no, nothing, thank you. I'm too upset to stay, anyway. I'm hardly in a 'party' mood." She got up, nodded to everybody, the trio of trustees just nodding back and mumbling good-byes.

Watching Brenda make her way back through the crowd, I spotted Glenda, the Goth box-office girl. She was alone, seated at a high-top table by the front windows, swirling her white wine in its glass, staring into it as if looking for omens.

I rose and snaked my way over toward her. On the trip, I overheard bartender June tell-ing a haggard blond woman at the counter, "Go home, Henny. You're already way over your limit."

"How 'bout one more for the road?"

"No. That's it, Hen. You're cut off."

Henny covered a burp, slid off the stool, steadied herself, smoothed her dress in a false stab at dignity, then tottered in the direction of the front door.

Please God, I thought, *don't let her be get-*

ting behind the wheel of a car.

Glenda was taking a sip of white wine when I came up alongside her high-top. "Hi, remember me? Brandy? The hat wrangler?"

Her heavily made-up eyes studied me. "Sure. You guys should have told me you were a comedy team. I might have sold more tickets."

"Well, we didn't know we were a comedy team till they started laughing, actually. All right if I join you?"

Glenda nodded toward the table of trustees. "Why? Bored with the company?"

I took the other stool. "You don't like them?"

She pursed her black-stained lips. "Bunch of stuffed-shirt hypocrites. Big deals in a little town."

"Does that include Chad? He's going to be a trustee, I hear."

"Chad's all right. He's young and he's smart and he's got talent. This town might finally see some changes, with him on the board."

"Is that right? My understanding is he told the trustees he plans to vote *against* incorporation."

A tiny smirk. "Yeah, that's what he *told* them."

214

"You mean, he has something else in mind?"

Glenda shrugged, sipped her wine. "Better ask him."

I tried another angle. "How did you wind up in Old York?"

"Born here. No way I'm dying here."

"Sounds like you don't like Old York very much."

"I don't. It's the worst."

"Why is that?"

"It's like living in a theme park, a crummy one. Or maybe a movie studio's back lot, fixed up like eighteen eighty. Soon as I get enough money? I am *vapor.*"

"How long will that take? Getting enough money, I mean."

A tiny black smile. "I'm workin' on it."

A waitress came over and I ordered a white zinfandel.

Then Glenda asked, "What's got Brenda's panties in a bunch? She flew out of here like her hair was on fire." She leaned close. "Couldn't be over her uncle, 'cause she didn't like him one little bit."

I figured Glenda would hear about Fred soon enough, so I told her.

"That's sick," she said, sounding sincerely sorry to hear the news.

"Did you know Fred well?"

A one-shoulder shrug. "Just from working part-time at the Vic. He wasn't much of a conversationalist. But he had hidden depths, ol' Fred."

"Really? How so?"

"Man, he was really talented. Just the kind of help a theater thrives on. That Fred could make *anything* — props, sets, you name it." A sigh. "If Chad keeps the theater going, replacing Fred is gonna be way tough."

"Fred was single?"

"Yeah. But I think he had something goin' on the sly."

"No kidding?"

"Yeah. After a performance one night? I saw him sitting in the parking lot, in his car, with some woman. Hangin' all over each other."

"Really! Who was she?"

Glenda shook her head. "Too dark to make out who he was makin' out with. And when they saw me, they took off in his car and she ducked down. So I figured she must be somebody's wife. That kind of stuff goes on all the time in these creepy little towns. Nothin' to do but . . . do it."

"Did you stay out in your box-office booth throughout the performance?"

She nodded. "I sit and listen to music and stuff, keep an eye on things."

"Well, do you know if any of the trustees left during our play?"

She cocked her head and some of her piercings slanted. "Why do you ask?"

I shrugged both shoulders. "I'd just like to know. I thought I saw somebody head out and not come back for a long time. Longer than a bathroom break. Struck me as really rude."

She accepted that. "Well, they're a rude bunch, all right, little tin gods. But no. A few people did leave — older folks who were offended by your act. You know, they were bitchin' — 'That's not Shakespeare!' That kind of thing. Sorry."

Understandable. Even I'd tried to leave. Even the table had.

"But you're sure that doesn't include any trustees?"

Glenda nodded. "I'm sure. I was in the ticket booth the whole time, and saw everybody who went out the front doors."

"What if somebody used the backstage exit?"

"The alarm would have sounded. Anyway, who cares if a few uptight fogies booked it? You were a smash." She downed the last of her wine. "Well, so much for my social life in thrilling Old York. I'm going home and hope my parents are already asleep." Glenda slid off the stool. "Nice talkin' to you, Brandy. You seem way cool."

"Try to be, within reason."

The waitress finally delivered my wine and I remained at the high-top, taking a sip and looking around the room for Mother. The trustees' after-party was breaking up, news of Fred's death obviously having put a damper on things. As Celia, Digby, Flora started glad-handing their way through the crowd, making a slow path to the front door, Mother materialized, holding a Shirley Temple and assuming Glenda's stool.

"Good call, dear," she said. "Buttonholing our lobby Goth, Glenda. Anything of interest?"

I gave her the gist, then Mother said, "Most distressing news, dear, if indeed none of the trustees left during the play. Do you believe the girl?"

"Why would she lie?"

"Why indeed. Why would anyone pierce her body and festoon what God gave her with metallic doodads? Did it occur to you perhaps that it was Glenda the Not So Good who left the theater and killed Fred?"

I frowned. "For some purpose, or just because it's good casting?"

Mother stirred her drink with the cherry, brought it up dripping and bit it off at the

218

stem. She chewed, swallowed, and said, "Suppose Glenda was blackmailing one of the trustees? You said the girl wanted money to leave Old York."

"Blackmailing a trustee over what?"

"Over poisoning Millie, possibly."

"And what? Fred found out?"

"Or," Mother said, really getting into it, "he was in on the blackmail scheme with her."

She had me nodding. "And why share the money with him?"

"Or maybe she was in on it with Chad."

"In on what?"

"A murder scheme to poison Chad's grandmother for the New Vic!"

"But it's falling down around everybody's feet."

"Ah, but the land would be valuable, particularly after incorporation."

She was making sense to me. Not really a good sign.

We sipped our drinks.

After a while, Mother asked, as if to herself, "And who was Fred Hackney's mysterious paramour? And where does she fit in? Whoever she is?" Suddenly she slipped off the stool. "Little girl's room! Won't be long. If the waitress comes by, ask for another round."

I was ready to leave, but Mother always had trouble calling it a night after a performance. And she was probably expecting Sheriff Rudder to call her cell phone.

Speaking of cells, I'd turned mine off when we got to the theater at six-thirty. I'd forgotten all about it, and now finally retrieved it from my little bag.

Tony had sent several texts: 6:44 pm, **Break a leg!**; 8:14 pm, **Hope the play went well**; 9:36 pm, **Heard about Fred. Call me!**; 10:12 pm, **Please call!**

It was now a little past eleven. I went outside with the cell.

"Brandy, are you all right?" Tony asked, his concern climbing through the phone.

"I'm fine. Sorry it took me so long to get back to you — I forgot my phone was off. How did you find out about Fred?"

"Rudder called me on his way to the church. Said Fred Hackney fell from a scaffolding."

"Mother and I and Father Cumberbatch found him."

"Was it really an accident?"

"I don't know, Tony. Mother's spinning all kinds of murder scenarios, but it just about has to be accidental. The doors were locked and the key Father Cumberbatch gave the man was still in his pocket."

He sighed. "You know this because Vivian picked his pockets."

"Well . . . she didn't keep it. What does Rudder think happened?"

"I haven't talked to him since he got to the scene, but it's likely he'll label it an accident, for the very reasons you mentioned."

"But three deaths in three days, Tony? In a town this size?"

"I know. One for Guinness. But it does happen. If these deaths had occurred in a town even the size of Serenity, nobody would think anything about it. Well, maybe your mother would."

"Anything yet on Barclay's autopsy?"

Silence, while he considered my request. "The coroner found a high amount of blood pressure medication in his system. Is there any reason why you can't head back right now?"

"We haven't spoken to Rudder yet."

"I'm sure he'd be happy to do that in Serenity."

"Sweetie, I'm really beat. We'll head back tomorrow afternoon, okay?"

"Make it tomorrow morning."

"Why does that matter, if this is just a bunch of coincidences, and not murders at all? Anyway, we're supposed to get our check from Chad around noon."

There was a long pause.

Then he said, "Because I'm a cop, honey, and cops don't believe in the Easter Bunny, Santa Claus, the Tooth Fairy . . . or coincidences. Please get your lovely self home."

"Okay. And in the meantime, I'll keep the gypsy's advice in mind."

"Huh?"

"Remember? Beware the Cyclops?"

The joke fell flat.

"Brandy, if your mother is right, and these deaths *are* murders, the killer is getting desperate. He's . . . it's what we call accelerating."

"I'll be careful."

"Move a dresser in front of your door tonight. Tell your mother to do the same."

"She'll be touched you care."

"Quite honestly, I would miss the old girl. You can even tell her that for me."

"Okay. Minus the 'old girl' part."

We said some smoochy stuff that is none of your business, and then I ended the call, returned to the pub, and found another glass of white zin and a Shirley Temple waiting.

Mother reached the table just as I did. She guessed whom I'd been talking to, and ordered me to repeat my conversation with

Tony, verbatim, the way Archie Goodwin does to Nero Wolfe. But I was no Archie. (*Reviewers:* It would be gratuitously cruel to quote me on that.)

When I'd finished my report, Mother said excitedly, "Now we *know* Barclay was murdered! He and Millie died by the same kind of overdose."

"We still don't know for sure that it's murder, Mother. Not for *certain.*"

She hit the table with an open hand, jostling our drinks. "This case is driving me bonkers!"

Medication can only do so much. Shirley Temples, too.

I slid off my stool. "Come on, honey, let's go. It's almost midnight. A good night's sleep will make things look clearer in the morning."

"You're right, dear. We need to recharge the little gray cells."

"Make up your mind, Mother. Wolfe or Poirot."

"Why not both?"

"How about neither?"

Leaving our unfinished drinks, we exited the pub.

Lights from the inn made a beckoning beacon across the village green, and we decided to cut through the park, where few signs of the fete remained, and were crossing Manchester Street when a single bright light shone on us and an engine roared.

A vehicle was headed right toward us.

Fast.

It swerved, not to avoid hitting us, rather to do a better job of it. I grabbed Mother's arm and propelled both of us forward, and we landed in the grass just as the car flashed by — too close for comfort!

At the end of Manchester, the vehicle took a hard left turn, tires squealing, and disappeared.

I got to my feet, then helped Mother up.

I asked, "Are you all right?"

She tested her legs. "Yes, dear. New hips seem to be working. Did you get a good look at the car?"

"No. Too dark, too sudden. Didn't get the color or license plate and certainly not a make or a model."

But I did notice one thing: the vehicle had only one headlight. What we midwesterners call a one-eyed car.

A Cyclops.

A TRASH 'N' TREASURES TIP

Most reputable dealers belong to an organization that holds them to high standards. In England, it's the British Antiques Dealers'

Association, or BADA. Mother thought their acronym held a negative connotation, and wrote suggesting that they change it to DABA. She's still waiting for their response.

CHAPTER NINE:
THE DEVIL CAN CITE
SCRIPTURE FOR HIS PURPOSE

You are in luck, gentle reader, and I am in luck, too, because this is Vivian speaking/ writing. I have only been assured one chapter per book — a limitation that goes back to my negligence in allowing Brandy to sign our initial book deal — but even my daughter cannot deny me center stage when that is where I am, and she herself is not present.

Thus I on occasion am given an additional chapter (in this instance, two and a half chapters!), and I am grateful to those of you who've taken the time and energy to write our publisher asking for more Vivian with a bold, tremulous hunger similar to Oliver Twist requesting more gruel.

Sunday morning, while Brandy and Sushi slept in, I thought it might prove comforting and perhaps spiritually uplifting to attend the eight o'clock service at the Episcopal Church, and take in whatever words of guidance Father Cumberbatch might impart to his followers in the aftermath of the multiple tragedies that had befallen Old York.

Of course, I also was curious to see if Sheriff Rudder and his men were still around, and if the sanctuary had been turned into a yellow-and-black-taped crime scene. Perhaps the service would have to be held outside. We certainly had a fine day for it, sunny but with a nice leaf-rustling breeze.

I arrived early, trying out a fall Breckenridge slacks and sweater outfit that I had purchased on sale, receiving another twenty percent off because it was the store's Senior Citizens Day (I was relieved to pass for over sixty-five, and anyway my driver's license ID had been revoked some time ago). The outfit was half a size too big, but it was doing the trick nicely. One never knows unless one tries!

Sidebar: I eschew dresses these days. The last one I bought had shoulder pads, and I mean circa the forties, not their revival in the eighties. (This is not to imply that *I* am circa the forties.) And nylons? Don't get me started. If it's bare skin some women don't like, why aren't they wearing nylons on their arms? Besides, after silk hose went out after WW II, what was the point? Not that I was around for WW II.

What was I saying?

Oh, yes. As I'd intended, I was the first to arrive for the service, and found a seat in the otherwise unoccupied sanctuary — a spot in the middle of the last pew on the right side of the aisle that would allow me a good vantage point for watching everyone as they came in.

Behind the pulpit, the scaffolding still stood in the apse (domed ceiling area); but the lack of yellow crime scene tape, and the apparent absence of Sheriff Rudder and/or his minions (no country patrol cars in the graveled lot, either), told me the sheriff was almost certainly treating Fred Hackney's fall as accidental.

Dropping like flies, all around us, and all our sheriff can do is find ways to excuse suspicious deaths. I was growing very disappointed with Serenity's sheriff. Perhaps next election I should run against him. Hadn't I solved every murder in the county for several years now?

Soon, others began to arrive, and among the first were the trustees. Celia and Digby wore somber expressions (although with Digby it could have just been his usual sour one) and walked down the aisle together as if they were disapproving parents in a wedding procession, but who had no choice due to a pending "blessed" event. The innkeeper-tress (that's not a real word but it should be) had on a navy dress with white collar, and the realtor a brown suit with tan tie. They sat in the second row on the left, in front of the pulpit. Apparently Celia's husband, Seabert, was either not religious or was back holding down the Horse and Groom fort.

Flora and Brenda arrived together, the former trading her usual titillating outfit for a conservative gray pants suit, while the latter wore a shapeless black dress, perhaps a nod toward mourning. They, too, sat near the front, but across the aisle from Celia and Digby.

I took note of the absence of certain others of interest, notably Chad, but also lobby-girl Glenda, barfly Henrietta, and the owners of the Red Lion, June and Marty. Their absences could be easily explained: Chad was of a generation that was a trifle godless, Glenda was probably sacrificing a goat, and the Red Lion owners had had a very late night dealing with the likes of Henny, who was probably lost in an alcoholic coma. Anyway, not everyone in the world is Episcopalian. I'm not!

As the congregation waited for the service

to begin, a low murmur filled the sanctuary — the death of Fred in this very space draped itself over the chamber like a dark, low-hanging cloud — and every so often an exclamation could be heard, as someone who hadn't been told about the tragedy was informed by another who had.

At a few minutes to eight, the congregation, anticipating Father Cumberbatch's imminent entrance, fell silent; and when, at precisely eight, he strode purposefully down the center aisle, everyone craned his or her head as he passed.

The priest, in a black robe with green stole cascading down each shoulder, moved solemnly to the pulpit; his face was drawn, even haggard, the events of the past few days having aged the youthful appearance. His eyes were bloodshot in a manner more suited to Christopher Lee in an old Dracula picture than a man of the cloth.

He looked out at his flock, his chin up.

"Please stand and sing the opening hymn."

I didn't have a program leaflet, having come too early for the greeter to hand me one at the door; but a board on the wall next to the pulpit listed what page to turn to in the hymnal book. Handy! I took the hymnal from its wooden rack before me and joined in singing "Amazing Grace," a church oldie but goodie (well, most hymns are, oldie I mean, though not necessary goodie), my stellar voice drowning out those around me. To inspire others, one must be a leader.

After the congregation was again seated, Father Cumberbatch began, "Today's scripture is taken from Matthew twenty-one, verses twelve through thirteen. 'And Jesus went into the temple of God, and cast out all those that sold and bought in the temple, and overthrew the tables of the moneychangers. . . .' "

Now I regretted having sat where I had, with such a limited view of mostly the backs of heads. Sometimes I outthink myself.

So I stood, and with some difficulty, began to slide down in the pew past my fellow parishioners, creating a few toe-casualties along the way. Really, my timing was off — if I had done this during the hymn, the hollers of "Owww!" and "Watch it!" might have blended in, or at least provided a percussive counterpoint.

As it was, enough heads swiveled in my direction to halt Father Cumberbatch in his scripture reading.

As I stumbled into the aisle, I filled the silence with, "Apologies, your honor!" For a panicky moment, I had reverted to traffic court mode — probably the priest's black robe.

"I *mean,* your eminence," I corrected, with a half bow. "Having difficulty hearing way back here — ear wax build-up, don't you know."

All eyes were on me, and I considered making a jest — "If this was a Pentecostal Church, maybe you could heal me!" — but thought better of it. One must consider one's audience.

I was heading down the aisle now and the silence followed me, and I felt the need to keep filling it.

"I'm afraid, Father, those over-the-counter ear wax remedies just never work out for me. I'm always misplacing that bulb thingie, which by the way works very well for watering small plants."

Around me were a few remarks that I will not report, other than to say none of them were very Christian.

"You'll find room in the first pew," the priest said with considerable resonance. Almost God-like, really.

"Oh. Well. I wouldn't want to sit *too* close." That way I couldn't even see *backs* of heads.

"Well, Mrs. Borne," he said with a smile that I thought seemed rather strained, "please land somewhere."

"Yes. Thank you. I will. There's always the stable!"

Crickets.

Why must churchgoers be so humorless?

Choosing the row behind Celia and Digby, I tried to squeeze into a spot on the aisle, but it wasn't big enough, so the man on the end had to scoot over into the woman next to him, and she pushed into the person next to her, and so on down the line, the way motorcycles parked too close together do, if the first one is knocked over.

Settled, I worked up an angelic smile for the priest — a good actress has the proper facial expression ready for any occasion. "You may resume."

"*Thank* you."

I gave the priest a mildly reproving look. Sarcasm has no place in the pulpit.

Father Cumberbatch cleared his throat. "And Christ said, 'My house shall be called the house of prayer, but ye have made it a den of thieves.' Let us pray."

Everyone bowed their heads, with one notable exception — myself. I recited along to the Lord's Prayer (FYI: the Episcopalians say "trespasses" instead of "debts"), but my head was turned and my eyes were taking stock. At the prayer's conclusion, Father

Cumberbatch stood silently at the pulpit, and he too seemed to study each and every face, before he spoke.

"Many of you have come this morning to better understand the losses of our fellow worshippers, Millicent Marlowe, Barclay Starkadder, and Fred Hackney. Why were they so cruelly taken from us?" He paused. "Some may say that it was God's will, His divine plan, while others may speculate that these souls were called to heaven because the Lord needed them at his side. But I will tell you nothing of the kind."

Murmurs among the congregation.

The priest went on: "Rather than try to find or invent meaning in their deaths, we should seek meaning in their lives — in the entertainment that Millie gave to the community through her love of the theater . . . in the history that Barclay celebrated and shared with us through his dedicated work at the museum — and in the helpfulness and hard work of Fred, who so often gave of his talents for little or no remuneration, which was what he was doing when, just hours ago . . . behind me where I stand . . . tragedy struck down this uncomplicated, generous man."

Soft sobbing could be heard around the congregation.

I had views of Celia and Digby, in front of me, and Brenda and Flora, to my left. The women were wiping tears with tissues or fingertips, but not Digby. He didn't even appear to be listening.

Father Cumberbatch was segueing into his sermon, Love Thy Neighbor, as stated on the board.

"The book of Mark tells us," he was saying, "to love our neighbor as ourselves. While God is to be loved above everything, our neighbor is above all others. And we are to extend to our neighbor the kind of love with which we treat ourselves. Leviticus tells us not to defraud our neighbor, nor to rob him, nor to seek revenge, neither to bear a grudge. Remember the Lord's teaching: 'All things whatsoever ye would that men should do to you, even so do unto them.' "

And here, dear reader, is where I fell asleep. I regret admitting this, because I found considerable value and wisdom in the young father's words. But I had stayed awake most of the night, watching TCM on the small tube television (thanks to Celia's hidden satellite dish).

This I had done not strictly because of the Robert Mitchum festival they were airing — though I do love that man! — but in case Sheriff Rudder might call. I knew darn well he would need my expertise to make sense of the crime scene, which is to say the very church I was seated in. But, alas, the obstinate man never phoned. I would write it off as his loss, but it was Old York that would suffer, since I felt convinced a murderer was on the loose.

A murderer very likely seated here in the sanctuary where his or her most recent homicide had been done. Hiding in plain sight among lesser sinners.

I was roused from my slumber by the final hymn, "The Church Is One Foundation," which was then followed by the closing benediction. Judging by the dirty looks the nearby churchgoers were flashing me, there may have been some snoring done.

The congregation stood and began its slow, shuffling exit.

As I moved into the aisle, someone behind me touched my elbow.

"Mrs. Borne?" a female voice intoned.

I turned to see a stunning woman in her midfifties, chicly dressed in a lavender tweed suit and beige patented pumps, her short black hair impeccably coiffed. She reminded me of Liz Taylor during her Passion perfume campaign. (I myself prefer White Diamonds.)

"Yes, I am Vivian Borne. And you are?"

"Edwina Kent." She gestured to the two women flanking her. "And this is Ivy Morton . . ."

Ivy, voluptuous in a too-tight green sheath dress seemingly designed to test the Lord's patience, looked like Marilyn Monroe if she had lived into her sixties and gotten off the booze and pills but perhaps had substituted pastries.

". . . and Melba Hornsby."

Melba, in a rumpled linen dress, was the spitting image of Marjorie Main, Ma Kettle herself, and so hilarious in the Fred Mac-Murray comedy, *Murder, He Says.* (Young people, that's what Google is for . . . and if you track that film down, you're in for a treat!)

"I'm pleased to meet all of you," I said with a little bow.

Designated speaker Edwina asked, "We wondered if you might like to join us for brunch."

I had hoped to arrange a time with Father Cumberbatch to query him on the details of our disappointment of how the county sheriff had handled Fred Hackney's "accident" last night. But by now there would be a long line of parishioners shaking his hand, and I could always track down the young priest later.

Besides, Edwina and Ivy and Melba presented a brand-new, possibly valuable source of information. After all, three women would hardly gather in order *not* to discuss town gossip.

I told them I'd be delighted to join them for brunch.

Shortly, we were piling into Edwina's white four-door Impala, to make the short drive to Ye Olde Tearoom on Brighton Street. On the way, Edwina told me that the three belonged to a women's group called the Juliets (Just Us Ladies Into Eating Together), and while the majority of Juliets were widows, like Ivy and Melba, a few, including Edwina herself, were not.

Edwina found a parking place on the street, and soon we were entering the small, quaint tearoom, whose decor was as charmingly Victorian as the building it inhabited.

Every table was full, and I was wondering about the wait, my stomach already growling like Sushi watching me eat potato chips without sharing, when a young, fresh-faced girl (excuse me! woman) in a crisp white waitress uniform came up to greet us.

"Your table is ready, Mrs. Kent," she addressed Edwina.

"Thank you, Hayley. Come, girls."

I trailed the Juliets across the room, then

down a side hallway to a back dining area, likely reserved for private parties, because no one else was brunching back here.

Hayley led us to a table with a white-lace-edged cloth, informing us she'd be back for our orders, then whisked herself away.

As we settled into chairs, Edwina, next to me, explained, "The Juliets have a special arrangement to take brunch back here every Sunday."

Ivy, on the other side of me, giggled. "We enjoy our privacy. We prize it! Being able to speak openly, I mean."

"If you get our drift," added Melba.

"I believe I do," I said with a smile. Once again I'd made a wise decision, trusting instincts well honed in the rumor mills of Serenity.

Menus were already on the table, along with filled water glasses, and two floral ceramic pots (one coffee, one tea). The silverware was not sterling, but high quality, the cups and saucers real china, the napkins linen. This simple elegance reminded me of Sunday dinners at my Aunt Olive's — before she died and was memorialized by way of having her ashes transformed into a paperweight. (That is, of course, another story.) (Available gratis at BarbaraAllan .com — such a deal!)

I seemed to be the only one studying the menu.

"What's good?" I asked, since it was clear everyone else was pre-decided.

"Oh, everything," enthused Ivy. Since she was on the plump side, I figured she would know.

"Pancakes are the house specialty," Edwina offered, with a smile that said she could already taste them. "They're so light, with fresh strawberries and a sprinkling of powdered sugar — ambrosia."

Melba said, "But I recommend the corned beef hash — none of that canned stuff. Strictly homemade."

Well, dear reader, as you might well imagine, I was all but drooling, so it was something of a relief to see Hayley reappear as quickly as she'd gone. Everyone (myself included) had the pancakes, except for Melba, who opted for the corned beef hash with poached eggs. And away Hayley went, our order in hand.

Edwina asked, "Tea or coffee, Mrs. Borne?"

"Tea . . . and please, call me Vivian."

Pouring for me, she said, "Vivian, first of all, we simply *must* tell you how much we love the books you and your daughter write."

"How very kind."

"Yes," said Ivy, little-girl breathy. "We've read every single one. The Juliets are something of a book club along with our other pursuits."

"How nice, dear."

"But we do have one complaint," Melba put in.

I managed not to frown. Readers need to learn that authors only want to hear what's good about their books, not what's bad.

I cocked an eyebrow. "Oh?"

"Yes," Melba continued. "We feel that you should take a greater hand in the writing. There are simply not enough chapters written by you."

"Don't get us wrong," interjected Edwina. "Your daughter's writing is perfectly fine, if rather pedestrian. . . . But you, Vivian, bring such keen intelligence and joie de vivre to your narrative, the words simply jump off the page!"

(*Brandy to Mother:* Okay, now, she didn't *really* say that.)

(*Mother to Brandy:* Are you calling my veracity into question, dear?)

(*Brandy to Mother:* Actually, I was calling you a darn liar.)

(*Mother to Brandy:* "How sharper than a serpent's tooth. . . .")

(*Brandy to Mother:* Tell you what . . . why don't I get this Ivy person on the phone and ask her if those were her exact words?)

(*Mother to Brandy:* Well, perhaps they weren't her *exact* words . . . but the gist of what she said is the same. If not the letter, the spirit!)

(*Brandy to Mother:* Bull hockey.)

(*Editor to Vivian and Brandy:* Ladies?)

(*Brandy to Editor:* We know, we know — knock it off.)

(*Mother to Editor:* But would you please consider Ivy's suggestion of more chapters by me? Hello? Are you there?)

Melba was pouring herself coffee. "I hate to admit this, Vivian, but I enjoy your books so much that I can't wait until there's another murder for you to solve. Is that terrible of me?"

I took a dainty sip from my china cup — good English tea. Perhaps we were a mite hasty in Boston back in 1773, throwing such good stuff overboard.

"Terrible or not," I said, "you might not have to wait long."

"You mean to say . . ." began Melba.

". . . that these deaths . . ." continued Ivy.

". . . weren't accidental?" finished Edwina.

"Isn't that what you already think?" I asked. "Isn't that why you really asked me to join you? In addition to requesting that I write more chapters in our books, of course."

(*Brandy to Mother:* Mother . . .)

(*Mother to Brandy:* Dear girl, let's not squabble. We'll wake the slumbering editorial beast again.)

As with the Romeos (Retired Old Men Eating Out) back in Serenity, all I had to do was get the ball rolling. Prime the pump. Goose the gander (not sure that's really an expression).

Anyway, Ivy was about to speak when Hayley appeared with the tray of our food, and no one said anything until after she'd distributed the meals — can't have witnesses to such conversations. Then the efficient girl (woman) was gone.

At which point Ivy whispered, as if the walls had ears (and no ear wax), "I wasn't at all surprised by Millie's death, considering her ill health. And when Barclay died, I thought it was just a coincidence — odd, strange, but a coincidence. He had a bad heart, too, you know. But now for Fred Hackney to go? *Something* has to be going on."

Edwina, also speaking sotto voce, said, "I'm not sure that this has anything to do with anything . . ." We all leaned in to hear better. ". . . but *I* think someone is black-mailing our esteemed trustees."

Ivy and Melba made utterances of surprise, but I had already suspected such a possibility. All I lacked was a blackmail motive.

"Don't tease us," Melba prodded Edwina. "Spill!"

"Well, Robert . . ." Edwina looked at me. ". . . he's my husband, and also the president of the branch bank here. Yesterday he told me in strictest confidence that Friday morning Digby Lancaster withdrew twenty thousand in one-hundred-dollar bills from his business account."

Melba shrugged, dismissive of this supposed revelation. "So? As a land developer, Digby must surely deal in large amounts of cash from time to time."

"But that's not all," Edwina said, like an infomercial pitch woman. "That very same afternoon *Celia Falwell* wanted a loan on the inn . . . for an identical amount!"

"Did Robert give her the money?" Ivy asked in her little-girl voice.

Edwina shook her head. "My husband told her he couldn't approve the loan because there's *already* a second mortgage on the inn. She didn't appear to know that, either. According to him, she left pretty unhappy."

Melba smirked. "And when Celia's un-happy, Seabert is going to be *really* un-happy."

"Sometimes I feel sorry for him," Ivy said softly.

"I feel sorry for Celia," countered Melba. "That Seabert is so *weird.* You won't *believe* what I saw him doing."

"What?" Edwina and Ivy asked.

Melba leaned closer, her eyes moving to each of our faces. "At about three in the morning . . . right outside the inn . . . he was changing the letters on that sidewalk sign of theirs."

My fork, halfway to my mouth with a speared piece of pancake, paused midair. "What was that, dear?"

She said, "I'm something of an insomniac, Vivian, and occasionally I go for a brisk walk on the green in the wee hours — Why the startled look? I'm quite safe. I always bring along a mace spritzer, and anyway, with this face I don't get hit on all that much, even in the daylight."

Especially in the daylight, I thought.

"Anyway," she was saying, "I was near the band shell when I glanced across at the inn, and what do I see? Seabert on his knees in front of that outside sign, changing the letters around!"

"You're positive it was him?" I asked.

"Who could miss *that* Ichabod Crane!" she snorted. "Anyway, it struck me as a strange time to be doing something like that. Strange time to be doing about anything."

Edwina shrugged. "Well, you were out walking. Maybe Seabert had insomnia, too. People have different ways of dealing with that."

I asked Melba, "Did you happen to see how he rearranged the letters?"

"No. Too far away. But he was doing it furtively."

I changed the subject. "Have any of you noticed a car around town with only one headlight?"

Ivy shrugged, Edwina shook her head, but Melba spoke up again. She didn't miss much, bless her.

"I've seen a one-eyed car on my nocturnal jaunts plenty of times — a dark blue Mustang."

"Do you know whom it belongs to, dear?"

"Sure. That sullen long-haired grandson of Millie's — Chad Marlowe."

Thanks to my considerable theatrical training, I was able to conceal my excitement.

"Vivian," Edwina asked, "are you leaving?"

Apparently I'd jumped to my feet. I sat back down.

"No, just a sudden gas pain. I'm fine." Improvisational skills come in so handy in detective work.

"What's significant about Chad's car?" Edwina asked, her interest piqued.

Since I didn't care to have Nancy Drew and her gal pals Bess and George interloping into my investigation, I said with a shrug, "Just that he should get it fixed. One-eyed cars can be dangerous."

Time to change the subject again.

"Edwina," I said, daintily using a napkin to remove the powdered sugar and maple syrup from my lips, and my chin, and one cheek, "you say you suspect blackmail — but what might the motive be?"

"Oh," the Liz lookalike said, "I have no idea."

Rats.

I asked, "Could someone be trying to buy pro- or anti-incorporation votes on the board?"

"Possibly," Edwina said. "Chad's vote might be for sale. I understand he announced at the impromptu board get-together Thursday night that he planned to vote no. But that could have been a sly way to attract offers."

Hayley arrived with our checks, Edwina graciously picking up mine.

While we waited for change, I casually remarked, "Speaking of Chad, I imagine the young man will be inheriting his grandmother's theater."

Edwina's eyebrows went up. "Yes, but that's about *all* he'll be getting."

"Oh? I was under the impression Millie was rather well-off."

"Not the case, anymore," she said. "Robert told me Millie's been pouring her own resources into that theater for years."

Melba said, "And I doubt Chad could get much for that building."

"Yes," Ivy agreed. "Who would buy a broken-down theater?"

But postincorporation that land would be valuable indeed.

I said, "I heard Millie left some money to the church in her will."

"That's no great secret," Edwina said with a nod.

"Do you know how much?"

She didn't, and neither did the others. And if this group didn't know, no one in Old York did, except maybe Millie's lawyer.

"Anyway," Edwina said, "just because a

248

will states that a certain party gets some money, that doesn't mean they'll get it."

"You mean," I said, "if there's no money to be had, you can't have any money."

"Truer words," Edwina said.

We left the table and made our way back through the hallway to the front, where business was slowing down.

Out on the sidewalk, Edwina announced, "Well, that was fun! Vivian, promise you'll join us any time you're visiting Old York."

"That you can count on," I said. Particularly if I was investigating a murder.

Edwina asked, "Can we give you a lift, Vivian?"

"No, thank you. After that sumptuous brunch, the walk will do me good."

But I'd stick to the sidewalk — no jaywalking, even in the morning. Not with that one-eyed vehicle on the loose.

We said our good-byes and parted.

With my mind abuzz with information I'd gleaned from the Juliets, I returned to the inn to tell Brandy.

In the lobby, Seabert was checking out a guest, and I waited till he'd finished and the guest had departed before stepping up to the counter.

"Mr. Falwell," I began pleasantly. "I'd like to ask a favor. . . ."

He could barely contain his irritation, but mustered an unconvincing smile. "Well, of course, I will do my best to comply, Mrs. Borne, although frankly I'm rather busy."

"Oh, I think you'll make time for me."

"Is that so?"

"It is. I'd like you to bring that outdoor sign of yours up to my room, along with its letters."

He jumped back a step. "What was that?"

I repeated my request.

He said, "Well, that's absurd. Why would you want me to do such a thing? And what makes you think I'd ever agree?"

"Because if you don't, dear boy," I said, allowing a bit of my Brit accent to come into play, "I'll tell one and all that it was *you* who wrote those nasty messages. Now chop-chop!"

I had no idea he could move so fast.

A TRASH 'N' TREASURES TIP

When buying antiques that you know little about, begin with inexpensive items. That way, if mistakes are made, they won't be costly ones. Mother's "vintage" Brown Betty teapot is adorable, but not worth the hundred dollars she paid, in part because it wasn't as vintage as she is.

CHAPTER TEN:
OUT, OUT, BRIEF CANDLE

Brandy again.

I had just finished dressing when I heard a commotion across the hall. It sounded something like a steamer trunk being hauled up the stairs, accompanied by groaning and muttering worthy of Marley dragging his chains in to see Scrooge.

Carefully I opened my door and peeked out and saw Seabert Falwell, lugging the inn's clunky outdoor sign up to Mother's door, where he paused to catch his breath before knocking. The hand clutching the sign's steel stem also held on to a white plastic sack whose bottom bulged, like a Halloween bag after a successful round of trick-or-treating.

Mother quickly appeared. "Well, *that* wasn't so hard now, was it, Mr. Falwell?"

His obsequious tone was tinged with malice. "Where would you like this, madam?"

I left a still-slumbering Sushi behind, went out and crossed the hall to see what this was all about. Actually, I had a vague idea, and if you've read any of our previous accounts — *Antiques Con,* for example — you may have one, too.

"Oh, good morning, dear!" Mother said from her doorway with a smile, craning around Seabert and his cargo to do so. "Lovely day waiting for us out there!"

The innkeeper, holding on to the sign sideways like a body he was dragging off somewhere, said, "Mrs. Borne? *Where,* please? This is heavier than you might think."

She withdrew into the room and I heard her say, "Over by the window will be fine. And just drop the sack of letters on the floor in front of it."

"Yes, Mrs. Borne," the innkeeper responded, despondently dutiful.

I joined them and shut the door behind me. Seabert glanced at me and winced at the thought of sharing his indignity further.

After he'd done Mother's bidding, the faux-Fawlty faced her. "I am humiliated and ashamed, madam."

"Please stop referring to me as 'madam,' Mr. Falwell. I'm beginning to feel like the proprietress of a bordello."

"I'm sorry. So sorry. Please let me explain my actions. . . ."

Mother tossed a hand. "No need. I quite understand your motive — you wanted to unsettle the trustees who had voted no on incorporation."

"Excuse me," I said. "What's going on here?"

Her eyes still on our hangdog host, she said to me, "Mr. Falwell was responsible for posting those unnerving messages."

"Not *all* of them," the innkeeper insisted defensively, eyes flicking briefly my way. "Not the ones about rotten rooms or horses on the moon. That was some prankster. But yes, the others, I did do."

I said, "Well, *those* were the nasty ones."

"Yes, and I do apologize. And, believe me, I wish I hadn't."

"I wish you hadn't, as well," Mother said. "Particularly considering that the suspicious deaths of Barclay Starkadder and Fred Hackney followed soon after."

Seabert raised his hands as if in surrender. "You're being most unfair, Mrs. Borne. Barclay died from a heart attack, and Fred's fall was accidental. My messages had *nothing* to do with what happened to them."

"My inquiries," Mother announced, "indicate both men were murdered."

253

His hands came down to settle on his chest, his eyebrows high over wide eyes. "You can't think *I* had anything to do with that!"

Mother studied him like a script page. "Not directly, no. But you may have inadvertently inspired someone to take advantage of your threatening messages — just as you were inspired to write them by some unknown prankster."

I knew she was just rattling his cage now. But that had been low of the man, posting those ominous messages after the deaths.

He lowered his head and folded his hands, holding them before him. He was outright pleading. "Please, please, in heaven's name, *please* don't tell Celia. She would kill me."

"Poor choice of words," Mother said.

It was no surprise that Seabert was more worried about his wife's wrath than what harm he might have caused. But then, if I were in his place, I might feel the same way.

"I see no reason to inform your wife," Mother said magnanimously. "Nor the authorities — unless a law enforcement officer questions me on the subject, and it becomes necessary."

His relieved sigh started at his toes and ended as it escaped through his pitiful smile. "Thank you, thank you, thank you. You are very kind, Mrs. Borne. Gracious beyond understanding."

"Well, let's not overdo it," Mother said. As if she hated overacting. Then, with a dismissive flip of the fingers of her right hand, she said, "You may go."

Seabert almost ran to the door, going out with Mother on his heels, and she closed the door right behind him.

"Do you buy that?" I asked.

"I do, actually. I don't believe that weasel has it in him to conceive of such an elaborate, nefarious murder scheme."

It occurred to me that I'd never heard anybody say "nefarious" out loud before, not even Mother.

I said, "Well, I agree with you, but not because he isn't capable of murder. After all, every time he looks at his wife, there's murder in his eyes."

"True," Mother allowed. "But then what makes you agree with me, dear?"

"If Seabert is the killer, he would never have posted those messages, calling attention to himself. And I doubt the real killer would take a chance, even in the middle of the night, of being seen rearranging those letters. Anyway, what would be the point?"

"Very impressive reasoning, my dear," Mother was saying as she adjusted the positioning of the sign near the window.

I nodded toward the thing. "I'm afraid I already have a sick feeling about why you blackmailed Seabert into loaning you that sign."

She sat on the foot of the bed, where the tilt she'd given the sign gave her a good view. "Dear, you *know* I can't concentrate sufficiently on a case without my incident board."

At home, she always used an old schoolroom blackboard on wheels to compile her suspect list. And on a recent trip to New York, where we attended a comics convention in the Hotel Pennsylvania, a lobby-café chalkboard sign went mysteriously missing. (Yep, *Antiques Con.*)

Mother was saying, "I'll give you a name, and you arrange it on the board with the letters."

"Mother — what, do you expect me to go down on my knees in front of that sign and empty the bag of black letters, and spread them on the floor and take dictation from you? That will take an hour!"

It took half an hour.

Now the board looked like this:

PRIME SUSPECTS

CELIA

DIGBY
FATHER C
FLORA

SECONDARY SUSPECTS
SE BERT
CH D
BREND
HENRI TT

(I eventually ran out of letters *A* and *E,* so you'll have to fill in those blanks yourself, mentally, just as Mother did.)

"How's that?" I asked, sitting back on my haunches.

Mother nodded. "Satisfactory."

She was doing Nero Wolfe again, but I doubted Archie Goodwin would have had the patience, much less the lack of self-respect, that it took to crouch for half an hour putting letters on that sign.

I went over to where she was seated on the bed and joined her. "Mind telling me where you were this morning? I had to take breakfast by myself."

"I meant to get around to that, dear," she said, eyes gleaming. "I attended a *most* interesting church service, then had lunch with some very knowledgeable local ladies."

Then Mother proceeded to tell me about

257

Father Cumberbatch's cryptic sermon (well, what she'd heard of it before dropping off) and how Sheriff Rudder had come and gone in the night, writing off the Hackney death as accidental.

Also, she informed me of Digby's twenty-thousand-dollar withdrawal from his bank, and Celia's failed attempt to get a loan for that amount, for imaginary repairs and renovations. Both pointed to a payoff of some kind.

Finally, saving the best for last, Mother revealed that Chad Marlowe drove a car with one working headlight.

"Chad?" I said. "Why would *he* want to run us down?"

Unless it was his idea of reviewing our performance last night.

Mother stood and smoothed her Breckenridge ensemble. "Well, we're supposed to pick up our check at the theater in a few minutes. Why don't we *ask* him?"

I said, "That could be dangerous. I spoke to Tony last night, and he said if there *is* a killer at large in Old York? That killer is getting desperate, and escalating."

"He did, did he? Well, I don't see Chief Cassato here at our side investigating."

"It's not his case."

"No, but his beloved Brandy is in the thick

258

of it. Why isn't he here protecting you?"

"Because I promised him we'd head home as soon as we get our check."

Behind the lenses, her eyes grew huge. Huger. "And you took it upon yourself to speak for both of us?"

"I did."

"And you imagined I'd comply?"

Not really.

"Anyway," she said flippantly, "who needs Chief Tony Cassato for protection? Sushi's sharp little teeth have come to our aid in more than one instance."

Right. Who needed a brawny, armed police detective when a ten-pound shih tzu was on the job?

I mulled it. "You know . . . Chad might figure out that we suspect him, if we don't go over and pick up our check. And we *do* still have to retrieve our hats. I mean, he can't run us over in his office, right? Particularly if we don't betray that we do suspect him."

"Exactly! Just act naturally, like me." She said that with a straight face, by the way.

I checked my wristwatch. "What about our rooms? It's already almost checkout time."

"We'll take care of that when we get back from the theater, dear. Anyway, I have the distinct feeling that Seabert will be lenient on that matter."

"We better take the car," I said, not wanting to walk back from the theater with the box of hats.

"Very good, dear. I'll meet you downstairs."

I returned to my room to get Sushi and her carry-sling, plus my little cross-over bag with car keys and cell.

Soon we were piling into the Ford C-Max in the parking lot behind the inn and taking the short drive over to the theater, where I parked in front.

The New Vic's lobby doors were locked, and a call from my cell to the office's number went unanswered.

"Let's go around back," Mother suggested. "Maybe the stage door is open."

It wasn't, but an outside staircase led to a door on the top floor.

Staring up there, Mother said, "Millie mentioned that Chad lives in an apartment above the theater." She gestured to the stairs. "Shall we?"

"What's the point? He's not here." I jerked a thumb at the empty graveled spot with grooved tire tracks next to the staircase.

Mother shrugged and said, "Perhaps Chad

moved his car in case we might recognize it."

"That's possible, Mother . . . but that's a long, steep climb to see if you're right."

But she was already a third of the way up.

And of course I followed. Several times we paused while she caught her breath — I took advantage of those stops, too, as Sushi was surprisingly heavy in the sling — but eventually we made it to the small outdoor landing with wrought-iron railing.

Mother knocked on the apartment door.

Nothing.

She knocked again — harder.

When that too brought no result, Mother tried the knob, which turned in her hand.

She threw me a wicked gleam. "You know what I always say about an unlocked door, dear."

I did. "It's an open invitation to enter."

"It surely is. And another thing I always say is, you can't break and enter when there's no breaking."

"But you're *still* entering. . . ."

Only she already had.

The door opened into a living room, decidedly male in decor: black leather couch and recliner, modern accent tables, and a massive entertainment center with all the latest toys. Chad's grandmother's reduced financial straits had had no apparent impact on the apartment above the theater.

And while the New Vic might lack technological advances, Chad Marlowe did not. His flat-screen TV alone was twice the size of ours.

We moved through the living room and down a narrow hallway, where we paused at an open doorway. The bedroom showed signs of hurried departure — dresser drawers pulled open and emptied, open closet cleared, some hangers askew, others on the floor, as if clothes had been ripped from them.

"As they say in jolly Old England," Mother said, "methinks Chad has done a runner."

She crossed to a corner wastebasket, knelt, and began riffling through it.

After a few moments, Mother exclaimed, "Ah-ha!"

She held up a handful of white and brown paper strips like she'd won the lottery.

She said, "Here are four bank wrappers, each labeling five thousand dollars in hundred-dollar bills. If these aren't from Digby's payoff, I'll eat my hat. I'll eat every hat in our Scottish play!"

"That doesn't make Chad a killer," I said, coming over for a closer look. "I'm not even sure it breaks any law, selling his vote on the board."

"However you spin it, dear, it makes him one heck of a person of interest!"

Her purse had been dangling from an arm, and she withdrew her cell phone.

"Hold it," I said. "Who are you calling?"

But the cell was already to her ear. "Sheriff Rudder? Thank you for taking my call. This is Vivian Borne. . . . Well, I'm sure you *do* have caller ID. Why do you think I thanked you for taking the call . . . ? Be that as it may, I need you to snap to and put out an APB on Chad Marlowe ASAP. Or is that a BOLO now? APB, BOLO, ASAP — just do it! . . . I am *not* overly excited. I don't remember ever being more calm. Now — look for a one-eye . . . What? No, Chad *Marlowe* doesn't have one eye, his *car* does. . . . Hello?" She looked at me astounded. "Can you believe that? He hung up!"

"Yeah. Really hard to believe." I knelt and Sushi and I looked right at her as she still hovered over that wastebasket. "Mother, we're going to need more than four bank wrappers to convince a knucklehead like Rudder that Chad is a killer."

"You're right, dear."

"Thank you."

"Rudder *is* a knucklehead."

263

I forged ahead. "We have to prove that Chad gave his grandmother an overdose of her medication, and did the same thing to Barclay, and that he then pushed Fred from the scaffolding. Assuming he committed all three murders."

She was nodding as I helped her to her feet. My thighs were still aching from squatting in front of that stupid Horse and Groom sign. Her knees popped like champagne corks.

"Dear, Chad had the opportunity in each instance." She counted off on her fingers. "He had access to Millie's medication. He helped set up the Tombola bottles. And he could easily have killed Fred using the back stairs of this apartment without Glenda seeing him go."

Holy box office, Batman — Mother was right.

Mother continued. "Furthermore, Chad had a motive for each." Again, she counted on her fingers. "Millie was running through his inheritance. Barclay, having refused to pay his extortion demand, threatened to expose him. And Fred —"

She stopped, her middle finger rudely in the air.

"I haven't figured out yet," she said, "why Chad killed Fred, but they were associates here at the theater, so maybe our handyman friend helped Chad by making sure Barclay won the poisoned beer, and thus became a loose end."

"That would be my best guess," I said, nodding.

"Then why do you look unhappy, dear?" Mother tilted her head. "Is something wrong? We're closing in on the killer!"

"Maybe we are. But because of who that killer *is,* now we're not going to get paid for doing the Scottish play."

I'd been looking forward to buying a pair of Kate Spade heels with my share of our performance fee, a potential purchase that had become even more important to me after my humiliating onstage hat-wrangling experience. Of course, a lot of people *did* like the show . . . so maybe there'd be future bookings.

"There, there, dear," she soothed. "Mother will fix that. I'm sure we can find some *other* form of remuneration."

"If you're thinking of taking something, that's what the police like to call stealing."

"I don't think helping ourselves to an item of like value is stealing at all." She shrugged. "Tit for tat."

An expression I never feel comfortable using.

I said, "Well, before we go unhooking Chad's Blu-ray player, or hauling out his flat-screen, we might want to poke around his office and see if our check is there. Short of that, some cash maybe."

"Good idea, dear."

Breaking and entering, felony theft — just another day in the life of Brandy and her zany mother.

Stairs behind a door at the end of the hallway took us down to the office on the first floor. And I took Sushi out of her sling and set her down while we poked around in drawers and file cabinets.

After a while, I asked, "Anything? I found a quarter on the floor."

"Nothing by way of covering our fee." Mother was seated behind the desk. She had an evil grin going. "But I *have* found Millie's address book, listing the trustees' phone numbers, which gives me an idea as to how to next advance our investigation."

She dipped into her purse for her cell and squinted at the address page, punching in numbers.

Soon she was saying, "Mr. Lancaster? Vivian Borne, here. . . . Fine, and you? . . . Good. I'm over at the theater and thought you might like to know that the artistic director has decamped. . . . That's right,

Chad's gone. . . . Well, as we say in the detective game, he's skipped, taken a powder, skedaddled, amscrayed, made a good and proper getaway. *And* with your twenty thousand, it seems. Or was his absence what you purchased? . . . Oh, well, I think you know very well what I'm talking about. . . . Such language, and on a Sunday! Mr. Lancaster, I just thought you might like to come over to explain your payoff, before I call Sheriff Rudder." She ended the call, then looked at me. "Make sure the front door is unlocked, dear."

Sushi scampering at my heels, I went out into the lobby, unlocked the center door, and returned.

About five minutes later, the land developer bulldozed in. Casually dressed in a green knit shirt and brown slacks, he strode up to the desk, behind which Mother still sat like a principal awaiting a recalcitrant student.

She had a chair opposite her waiting for him and gestured to it. He sat, heavily. Well, he probably always sat heavily.

Digby demanded, "What makes you think I gave . . . *how* much did you say? Twenty thousand dollars? To Chad Marlowe? That's ridiculous."

Mother placed the bank wrappers on the

desk. "These were in Chad's wastebasket."

Digby stared at the wrappers. "So?"

"So you withdrew that amount in cash from the local bank, and we can prove it. If you don't tell me the reason why you gave twenty thousand dollars in hundred-dollar bills to Chad Marlowe, I will feel obligated to turn these wrappers over to Sheriff Rudder, who I am sure will find them of interest in his ongoing investigation into the deaths of three people."

Digby swallowed, but then waved off Mother's little speech. "That money was a donation to the theater."

Mother leaned forward, tenting her fingers. "I see. Well, very generous of you, but nonetheless alarming to hear. You see, that means the young man has absconded with your donation. We should phone the sheriff straightaway, don't you think, Mr. Lancaster?"

Shifting in his chair, he said, "I *meant* to say the money was a *personal* gift to Chad, with no strings attached. No law broken in his leaving town with it."

I said, "Mr. Lancaster, do you know Glenda, the girl who works in the box office here?"

He glanced at me as if surprised I had the power of speech. "I know who she is.

Wouldn't say I *know* her."

"Well, she knows Chad, very well. She implied strongly that Chad wasn't truthful when he stated his 'no' position on incorporation to the trustees. That his real intention was to let certain board members — including you — understand that his vote was for sale."

The man's face reddened. "What some idiot girl *implies* — some creature whose head would set off an airport metal detector — means nothing to me, or anybody."

Mother said, "Come now, Mr. Lancaster. Brandy and I saw you and Chad together after that informal board meeting Thursday night. You approached Chad with the offer, didn't you?"

"You're out of your mind."

"Yes, so I've been told. So perhaps in my confused mental state, I have it backward. Chad approached *you* . . . and Celia and Father Cumberbatch. *Every single one of you* had to kick in if you wanted to buy his precious vote. That makes a sixty-thousand-dollar fresh start for Millie's sweet grandson."

"Absurd. And, anyway, if you were right, what crime would there be to it?"

"Chad selling his vote, in a position of public trust, is indeed illegal . . . and if you conspired with Celia and Father Cumberbatch, Mr. Lancaster? You'd be in the next cell."

He sprang to his feet, and his eyes were so tight, they were slits. "Good-bye, Mrs. Borne. I hope you and your daughter had a lovely time in our little town."

The realtor walked briskly to the office door, paused, then looked back. "But if you tell the sheriff about the cash I gave Chad? I will swear it was a personal gift, and no one will ever be able to prove otherwise."

After we heard the lobby door slamming, I asked Mother, "Don't you think he should have been more upset about Chad taking off with his money?"

"No, dear. You see, by leaving town, Chad has relinquished his spot on the board. So, either way, Digby gets what he wants."

Mother plucked the wrappers off the desk, put them in her purse, then stood at the chair and stretched, bones popping like corn.

"Come along, dear. Let us sally forth to the theater's prop room, to seek remuneration for our services."

Murder case or not, an actor will be paid.

She was coming around the desk when I stopped her.

"Hold on, Mother. We need to be very

careful how we go about this."

"Oh?"

"Yes. There could be some valuable antiques in there, on loan from the museum. Like those swords Brenda mentioned."

"If there are, dear, with our antiques expertise, we'll be able to identify them as such, and pass them by. And I certainly have no interest in those swords, however valuable. After all, I'm no thief!"

While Mother headed off to the prop room backstage, I went to reclaim our hats from the dressing room, which was just down the hall. There, I found a good-size cardboard box and loaded it up, then left it behind while I went to check on Mother.

Since Sushi was not with me, I assumed she had followed Mother, as Soosh adores any theater prop room. No, our pet does not have show business in her blood, she's just attracted by unusual smells.

In the cramped, stuffed-to-the-rafters prop repository, Mother was filling her own box. Not trusting her judgment — really, not trusting *her* — I rummaged through her "remunerations" to make sure nothing looked like it should be locked behind glass in a museum. Nothing qualified. Her picks were mostly items that would likely end up in another prop room, the one back at

Serenity Playhouse.

"Those *are* handsome," Mother exclaimed, pointing to two medieval swords with jewel-encrusted handles that were resting on an old trunk.

I said, "Must be the swords on loan from the museum."

Mother picked one up, hefted it, then shook her head. "No, I don't think so — not heavy enough. An excellent replica, but not the real thing. Definitely a prop."

"Really looks great."

She examined it closer. "Look here, dear. . . ."

Mother was pointing to where the blade met the handle, and the letters *FH* were visible.

"Fred Hackney," I said.

"I noticed several props carried his hallmark — he was a real artist. Who'd have guessed?"

Right then I noticed something, too, and a tiny spike of panic went through me. "Mother . . . where's *Sushi*?"

"I thought she was with you, dear."

"No. I thought she'd be in *here,* having a field day."

"Not to worry, dear," Mother said, replacing the sword on the trunk with its mate, "the little darling knows her way around a

272

theater."

"Not this one," I said.

I hurried out into the hallway, called for her, called again, and suffered that terrible sick feeling a pet owner gets when their precious little family member is missing. I called several more times, and finally was very relieved to hear a muffled bark.

A series of such barks led me to the workshop area, where I spotted a familiar little bulge behind a backdrop hanging on one wall. Pulling back the curtain, I found Sushi with her nose pressed against the wall.

"Find a rat, did you?" I said. Vermin and old theaters went hand in hand. And doggies went nose to nose with vermin.

"Come here, rascal," I commanded.

But the little mutt stayed put, rooting against the wall.

Bending to scoop her up, I noticed a sweeping half-circle scratch in the wood floor as an ill-fitted door might make when opened.

"What are you doing?" Mother asked right in my ear, and I jumped.

"Don't *do* that!"

"Do what, dear?"

"Scare the stuffing out of me." Only I didn't say "stuffing." My hands were moving vertically down the wall. "There's a

273

seam here. . . ."

Then my fingers found a small metal button, which I pushed, and a panel popped open about a half an inch.

"A secret door," Mother exclaimed. "Just like in a dark old house movie! How delightful!"

My fingers got under the opened edge, and as I drew the door wide, its bottom scraped along the floor.

Stone steps led down into darkness.

With girlish enthusiasm, Mother said, "Let's find out where it goes! If there's another exit, that would change all of our thinking."

I was about to discuss that with her when Sushi darted by, disappearing down the steps.

My frantic calls for her to come back were met with silence.

"Now we *have* to go down there, dear," Mother said. "No discussion necessary. I'll fetch a torch."

She meant flashlight, but the only one on the workbench was the dead flash I'd been given to locate hats in the dark. But we did find some candles and matches, and took those.

Before we committed to the Sushi hunt, however, I made sure the door could be opened from the other side, while Mother — taking an extra precaution so we all wouldn't be entombed — propped the panel door open with her purse.

And down we went, Mother maddeningly counting each step out loud, twenty-one in all. At the bottom, we halted, our candle flames flicking from a slight breeze caused by the open door above. Ahead, a narrow passageway, forged from the rock, stretched into blackness.

"The *tunnels* do exist!" Mother said. "Just as Millie said — like the real Old Vic!"

I called out to Sushi and my echo called back.

And so did a quick, sharp bark.

With Mother behind me, I moved forward slowly on the uneven cobblestone floor, my candle illuminating only a few yards ahead.

As Sushi's beaconlike barking told me I was growing ever closer to her, a sudden rush of air blew through the passage . . . and my candle went out!

Had another tunnel door opened some-where?

I stumbled badly, belly-flopping to the hard stone floor, where I lay stunned.

Had I tripped over Sushi?

Mother, her candle still lit, loomed over me, the angles of her face highlighted in orange. "So he didn't leave town, after all, dear."

I rolled over and looked into the open but very dead eyes of Chad Marlowe.

A Trash 'n' Treasures Tip

Over time, items that have been donated to theaters for set-dressing and props can become valuable and should be insured against fire or theft. On the other hand, when Mother tried to insure her vocal chords with Lloyd's of London, the Serenity Playhouse refused to pony up the $27.50 per annum.

CHAPTER ELEVEN:
IS THIS A DAGGER WHICH I
SEE BEFORE ME?

Scrambling to my feet and backing up, I bumped into a rock wall, but at least I didn't scream. Still, I think looking into the dead eyes of a corpse excuses any girly reaction I might have had.

Mother came over and lighted my candle with hers — I'd somehow managed to hold on to mine.

"Well," she said, "I guess that rules out Chad."

"Mother," I said, my breath coming tremulously, "we need to get out of here. The real killer could be *anywhere.*"

"My instinct is our culprit has fled. Let's take a moment to gather ourselves — all right? — and have a closer look."

Swallowing, I went over and knelt and held a candle over Chad's body, the flame leaping in my unsteady hand. Sushi was staying close beside me. I thought she might go over and start sniffing the body, but she didn't. Mother crouched and examined the fatal wound on the young man's chest, not touching it, eyes only. In Chad's limp right hand was a weapon, a revolver.

"He's been stabbed," she concluded, and gestured for me to give her my free hand, which I did.

Helping her to her feet, I asked her, "Any idea how long ago that was?"

"About twelve hours, judging by the advanced stage of rigor mortis. So I was right in assuming our murderer is long gone."

My nerves were settling. "Well, obviously, this must have happened *after* Chad tried to run us down last night."

In the flickering candlelight, Mother's narrow-eyed expression was all grooves and angles. "If indeed it *was* Chad behind the wheel. Any of our suspects could have been driving."

I pointed. "What about that gun in his hand?"

"A prop gun, dear."

"It certainly looks real."

"It is, in a way — it's a blank pistol. We've used them at the playhouse, remember?"

Such fake weapons used plastic wads instead of bullets, but could be just as deadly if shot at close range. Gifted actor

Brandon Lee lost his life that way, and others have, too.

I asked, "Do you know if it's been fired?"

"Not without examining it. Bend over and sniff the barrel, dear, but don't touch it."

"You want *me* to bend over and sniff the barrel."

"I believe that's what I said. Or perhaps there's an echo down here."

Mother rarely employs sarcasm, so I knew she meant business. I knelt. Sniffed. Something brushed my cheek and gave me a start — Sushi! Seeing me sniffing that gun barrel made her think she missed something, and she had a brief sniff, too, then backed away, unimpressed.

"I don't smell anything," I said, "and neither does Soosh, apparently. That thing must not have been fired, although if Chad's been dead for twelve hours, maybe I wouldn't smell anything by now."

"Oh, I think you would," Mother said. "You'd still get a pungent scorched bouquet. And Sushi would be down there sniffing away."

We were a few feet from the body, regarding it in the orange glow of our two candles. The dead artistic director did not seem exactly real. But he was. He was.

I asked, "What do you think happened here?"

Mother, not missing a beat, replied, "The theatrical gun indicates that Chad didn't trust whomever he was meeting in the tunnel, so he took along what was handy, in the prop room." She paused. "But it may have backfired on him — metaphorically, not literally."

"How so?"

"The prop gun is so realistic looking, it may have inspired the killer to strike first."

I was frowning and my stomach was going up and down, as if it were at the end of a diving board, trying to get the nerve to jump in. "Mother? There's something *really* upsetting about this. . . ."

"Well, of course there is, dear. Murder is always upsetting, particularly to the victim . . . unless of course it occurs before the victim knows what's happening."

"That's not what I mean."

"Oh. Well, finding Chad this way gave *me* a start, too. Think nothing of it."

"No, that's not it, either."

Mother cocked her head. "What then?"

"I'm afraid we've been sticking our collective noses into homicides so often these past few years, with Sushi part of the mix, that we've turned her into a . . . a *cadaver* dog.

280

That wasn't a rat behind the wall she smelled, it was Chad."

Mother shrugged, unconcerned. "Well, the poor dead boy *was* something of a rat, but I do get your drift. Might I suggest, however, that we table this discussion to a later, more opportune time?"

"Good point. Anyway, you need to call Rudder."

She nodded. "I believe there would be no harm in that. I've seen all I need to."

Since Mother had left her cell phone in her purse, propping open the door to the passageway, I got my cell out of my little bag. But down here deep in this tunnel, I couldn't get a signal. So I reached down to pick up Sushi, who'd been sticking close to me, tucked her in the carrier, and we retreated topside.

There, we extinguished our candles, and Mother retrieved her phone, though she left her purse in place as a doorstop.

"Sheriff Rudder? Vivian here."

She had him on speaker for my benefit, so I heard him growl, "Yes, I know it's you, Vivian. I saw the caller ID again. What is it now?"

"Might I suggest you pack an overnight bag?"

"What?"

"There has been another suspicious death."

"People pass away every day, Vivian, and there's nothing inherently suspicious about it."

"Well, it's inherently suspicious if they've been stabbed to death, isn't it?"

"If this is some kind of a sick joke, just to lure me there to listen to your crackpot theories —"

I spoke up. "Sheriff, this is Brandy. It's no joke. Chad Marlowe has been stabbed and he's dead all right, probably for ten or twelve hours. We discovered him in the tunnel under the theater."

A long pause while he tried to process all of that. "Tunnel? What are you talking about, a tunnel? Under the *theater*?"

"We didn't imagine it," I said. "It's quite real. Just get to the New Vic as soon as you can. A lobby door will be unlocked, and we'll be backstage."

Mother asked the cell, "Where are you, good sir?"

"Where do you think, Vivian? Serenity."

"So we should expect you in around an hour?"

"More or less."

"Thank you, Sheriff. Your professionalism is most appreciated." She clicked off.

I put my hands on my hips. "I *know* that voice — what are you up to? Appreciate his professionalism — are you kidding?"

She gave me that eyebrows-lifted, imperious look. "Why must I be 'up to' anything, child? Must I *always* be up to something?"

"Apparently," I said, and I would swear Sushi, riding my chest, nodded.

Mother shifted her stance. "I merely inquired about the sheriff's ETA because I wanted to know how much time we'll have to explore the tunnel."

Now my eyebrows lifted. "How much time we'll have is irrelevant, because there is no way we are exploring *any* tunnel. There's a dead man down there!"

"Who can obviously do us no harm." She put a hand on my shoulder, and Sushi frowned suspiciously. "Dear, you know very well that our sheriff will close that tunnel off as a crime scene — a crime scene that we will be forbidden to visit. The hour the sheriff has given us —"

"He didn't 'give' us an hour. He's an hour away!"

"The hour the sheriff has *provided* us represents our only chance to see where that tunnel leads."

"What if the killer is still down there?"

"After twelve hours? Highly unlikely, dear."

I was shaking my head. "I'm not going back down there. It's dark and it's creepy and it's dangerous."

Sushi was listening in her carrier, her head ping-ponging between us.

Mother sighed. "Very well. Your mother will go by herself."

"Bye."

"Perhaps you feel a woman of advanced years with artificial hips and limited eyesight will be perfectly safe, mounting such an endeavor."

Mother playing the age card — she *was* desperate.

She relit her candle, walked to the tunnel door, and paused dramatically. "Farewell, dear. Let me look at you and that darling dog for a moment. Fix you in my mind."

Sushi, wanting to go with Mother, was trying to squirm out of the carrier.

I put the dog down and she scurried over to her other mistress, eager for adventure.

"You two have fun," I said.

"Fun isn't the goal," Mother said. "Stopping a fiend is."

"Brother, Mother. You're really pulling out the stops. Okay, all right, let's go!" I took my candle over to Mother, relit it off hers, and followed her back down the stone stairs.

As we walked, the light of our candles played eerily off the walls.

"Why do you suppose this tunnel was put in, Mother, and when?"

"Possibly when the theater was built, as part of the effort to mirror the original Vic's tunnel system."

Orange and yellow ghosts danced along the rocky passageway.

I asked, "Where do you suppose it leads?"

"That's what I hope to discover. The Old Vic originals were British railway lines dating to the eighteen hundreds."

"Surely there must have been a more practical reason for the construction of this tunnel than duplicating the real theater."

It was like the places where the rough walls embraced our candle glow were on fire, as if we were walking down a flaming passageway.

"Well, in Prohibition days," she said, playing tour guide, "Old York was said to have done quite a bootleg business. I believe the Horse and Groom was a rather notorious speakeasy pub, back then."

"I would think this went back longer ago than that."

Mother shrugged. "Possibly. Perhaps it was part of the Underground Railroad.

Abolitionists were active in Iowa, way back when."

We were to Chad now. Mother gave him barely a glance, though as she passed, she did say, "Pardon us," and make the sign of the cross, even though she wasn't Catholic. I couldn't keep from looking at the poor young corpse as I skirted it, Sushi craning for a look from the carrier.

We pressed on for perhaps five minutes, then came to a circular area about twelve feet in circumference, off of which three more tunnels flowed. Our candle flames jumped and danced on the irregular walls as we turned in a circle, taking it in.

"We could get really lost doing this," I warned. Sushi was getting squirmy, so I set her down. She'd stay close to us.

"Not if we're systematic," Mother replied confidently. "We'll explore the right tunnel, come back to the circle, then take the middle tunnel, come back, and finally the left one."

"Okay. But if there are off-shoots? We don't follow them, all right? Mother?"

"Agreed."

We started into the tunnel on the right of where we'd emerged, and I took the lead, shielding my candle flame with a hand. Sushi was right behind me, and Mother brought up the rear. I did not relish taking point, but it was one way to make Mother keep her word, should an off-shoot tunnel present itself.

We moved slowly, the tunnel at times becoming more narrow, the walls even rockier, and I fought an ever-increasing feeling of claustrophobia. After about ten minutes of this, with me about to suggest turning back, stone steps suddenly rose before us.

"Wait here," I told Mother. "Let me scout ahead, all right?"

"All right. But be careful, dear. Stay close to the candle. The stairway can be . . . *treach*-erous."

"Mother, no *Young Frankenstein* quoting. None."

"It just came out, dear."

"Well, don't. Sushi, stay!"

The dog did as I asked for once, huddling near Mother's shoes.

At the top of the stone stairs was a wooden panel, about four feet by four. My free hand searched its edges for a button similar to the one on the theater's tunnel door, but found none. Pushing on the panel brought no results, either, nor was there any way I could find an edge to pull it toward me.

"Try sliding it, dear. That always works in

the Bowery Boys movies."

Mother was standing a few steps below me, Sushi just behind her.

"Mother!" I said. "Don't scare somebody at the top of stone stairs with no banister!"

"A banister would indeed be difficult to carve from stone," she said reflectively.

Why do I bother?

My sigh was half shudder as I handed her my candle, then placed both hands flat on the panel, and it slid easily to the left. Maybe I'd have known that if I'd ever seen a Bowery Boys movie.

I ducked and went through, and found myself behind the altar of the church.

Mother, having joined me, whispered, "I suspected we were heading in this direction."

I whispered back, "You know what this means. . . . Chad wasn't the *only* one who could have left the theater without being seen. Anyone who knows about these tunnels could have sneaked over here and dealt with Fred."

"Yes, dear. I've made similar assumptions. We mustn't tarry — the sheriff is on his way."

The trip back to the central circle was quicker, and Mother took the lead as we entered the middle tunnel. I was happy to have her do so. With our candles held before us, the orange-tinged passageway was gradually revealed before us.

This time we walked for about five minutes before coming to another flight of stone steps.

"Allow me," she said.

I gave her a mock-gracious "after you" gesture, and she went up while I waited at the bottom, Sushi pacing at my feet.

What seemed like another five minutes was probably under two by the time she came back down, probably quicker than was wise with her sketchy knees. But she was really into it.

"Well?" I asked.

"*Another* panel, dear, and it was probably a sliding one, as well."

"Probably? Didn't you slide it open?"

"No reason to. I could hear Celia talking on the phone. We're beneath the inn."

I frowned. "I don't remember seeing Seabert at our performance, do you?"

"No. I believe Celia said he stayed back to watch the front desk and otherwise tend to things." She paused. "Or I should say, he was *supposed* to. Certainly, as you are no doubt thinking, Seabert could have used this tunnel to get to the church and dispatch

Fred and return to his more mundane duties."

For a second time, we returned to the center circle, with a growing familiarity. We began the exploration of the left tunnel, with Sushi taking the lead, as if she knew it was her turn.

We walked for about eight minutes, splitting the difference between the time it had taken to traverse the right and middle tunnels. Finally we came to the expected stone steps, and it was my turn again. I climbed while Mother waited with Sushi.

At the top was a door with an easily found button, similar to the setup in the theater. After plastering an ear to the wood, listening for any noises behind it, and hearing nothing, I pushed the button, and the door swung outward with something of a groan and a scrape, as if it were a particularly heavy one.

I went on through and, as I turned to help Mother through, Sushi scampering by, I realized that the door on this side was cleverly disguised as a bookcase, shelves filled with leather-bound volumes.

"Where are we?" I whispered.

"The library room in the museum," Mother replied. "And we need not whisper — the place isn't open for another hour."

I nodded, taking in the opulent space. In addition to the floor-to-ceiling bookcases, a large fireplace took up much of one wall with lovely antique furnishings spotted around, including several Queen Anne couches, heavy ornately carved chairs, various Victorian lamps, and even a grand piano.

Mother had told me that the museum was once the home of one of the original trustees — a very wealthy one, at that — and the furnishings had been preserved to provide a snapshot of that earlier time, albeit with some updated electrical pieces.

Mother was saying, "While we're here, I want to go upstairs. There's something I simply *must* see."

"Well, you can see whatever it is after the museum opens. Right now, we need to get back to square one — the theater. Rudder could show up there any time. It would be nice to be able to make him think we were waiting there all the while."

"This won't take half a tic, dear." She was already moving across the oriental carpet to the library entrance, where a red velvet rope kept out visitors.

I grabbed up Sushi and followed.

Mother unhooked the rope, we all passed through, and she rehooked it.

I followed her up a wide staircase to the second floor, where we entered what must have been a bedroom at one time and now housed various antiques collections — here china, there pottery, and so on.

Mother stood for a moment, scanning the room slowly like a lighthouse beacon, then crossed to a wall of shelves protected by another velvet rope strung between two metal posts. As she proceeded to unhook the rope, I hurried over.

"What are you *doing*?"

Ignoring me, she went to a shelf, removed an article, and brought it back to show me.

With a wicked smile and an arched eyebrow, she asked, "Does this look familiar, dear?"

I barely gave the mahogany box with copper bands a glance. "No! Put it back. That's probably very valuable."

"Well, it's supposed to be, anyway." She turned it over. "Perhaps *this* might ring a bell."

One finger pointed to tiny initials carved on its bottom.

I had been holding Sushi, and put her down to take a closer look.

FH.

"Fred Hackney," I said numbly. "Oh my Lord — it's a fake! How did you *know*?"

Mother's smile was triumphant. "I noticed pieces of mahogany and copper on Fred's workbench when I fetched the candles."

"What's a fake doing on display in a museum?"

"Why indeed?"

I frowned. "Then . . . where's the *real* box?"

"Sold for a profit into someone's private collection, undoubtedly, with this impressively crafted imposter put in its place. How many more fakes are behind velvet ropes all around this museum remains to be seen — but my guess is, plenty."

Mother's eyes moved from my face and across my shoulder. "Well, Brenda, good morning. Or is it afternoon by now?"

I turned, and in midturn what I saw appeared to be a ghostly vision, as if someone out of a distant past had materialized before us.

But it was just Brenda Starkadder, wearing a voluminous eighteenth-century blue gown and a large black plumed hat, poised in the doorway. Had she been there long enough to hear us?

Mother, too cheerful, said, "I was just showing Brandy this magnificent tea box. Must have cost someone a pretty penny once upon a time."

"Is that what you were doing," Brenda said flatly, nothing of a question in her tone. She came toward us, the full fabric of the dress rustling like curtains in a high wind.

Stopping about three yards from us, the woman demanded, "How did you get in? What are you doing here, before we've opened?"

She must have already been up here on the second floor, and didn't know we'd come through the tunnel.

Mother replied, "Well, dear, we slipped in by the front door. I wasn't aware you didn't open until *later* on Sundays, and we were just leaving town, so . . . I'm afraid we just took advantage of that unlocked door. I hope you'll forgive us. Brandy, Sushi . . . let's be on our way."

Brenda shook her head, the plumes on her big hat waving. "Stay put. That door is locked. You're trespassing. And it appears you're stealing, too."

Mother shrugged. "Well, that door *couldn't* have been locked, dear. You must be mistaken. Because here we are!"

"Here you are," Brenda said.

I said, "We do apologize. We can postpone leaving town and come later. Mother, if you'll just put that beautiful tea box back, and yes, you're right, it *is* lovely."

The woman came closer. "As long as you're here, and fascinated by artifacts, perhaps you girls might be interested in this. . . ."

Her hands had been at her sides, hidden in the lush folds of the dress, but now her right hand emerged with a double-barreled pistol clutched in it.

Sushi, at my feet, gave a low growl.

Holding the weapon casually, Brenda said, "This antique gun is nine inches in length, has a solid silver handle, and was made in Birmingham, England, by B. Woodward and Son, around eighteen fifty. It's valued at around one thousand dollars. Oh! And it fires two shots."

"Antique firearms," Mother said, "aren't really our area of interest. But thank you for sharing."

"You know," Brenda went on, her eyes strangely distant yet very alert, "I'm always here a good hour early. I put on my costume when I arrive, and then I take a brief spin around the facility, to make sure everything is as it should be."

"Sounds like a wise procedure," Mother said.

"But it was just sheer luck, Sherlock, that I happened to be in the weapons room when I heard voices up here. And, suspecting there were burglars, I took this gun along for protection. Upon entering this room what should I find?" She nodded at the tea box in Mother's hands. "You two meddling oddballs, caught in the act of stealing a valuable antique."

As Brenda leveled the gun at us, Sushi darted forward and burrowed under the dress, which the woman lifted with her free hand, looking down with wild eyes as the dog's sharp little teeth latched on to her ankle. Fortunately for Brenda, and unfortunately for us, she was wearing leather high-button shoes, and the shih tzu's grip had no apparent effect.

Brenda shook Sushi off, snarled at her, one beast to another, and Soosh ran from the room, her nails heard clicking on the wood stairs as she dashed down, heading most likely for the tunnel. Maybe Sheriff Rudder would be at the other end by now, and maybe Sushi was smart enough to lead him here, if he was smart enough to follow.

Stalling for time, I announced, "You can try to float that story. But we know everything. And in this day and age, you can't shoot us and hope to get away with it. Intruders have rights, too, you know."

Brenda arched an eyebrow. "I'm prepared to take my chances . . . though when you say you know 'everything,' I have no idea what you might be talking about. Perhaps you'd care to enlighten me."

Since I was bluffing, I looked at Mother. Even in the face of death, the great diva knew how to pick up a cue, and how to hog the spotlight.

"Why don't I begin with Millie?" Mother asked Brenda.

The faintest smile tickled Brenda's lip as she trained the double-barreled weapon at Mother and me. "It's your story, Mrs. Borne."

Mother drew herself up. "Very well. It all began with Millie's accidental death, didn't it?"

I blurted, "What? Millie's death was an *accident*? Mother, you've called it murder from the beginning!"

"Yes, but we're at the ending now, dear — isn't that right, Brenda? Millie's accidental death, the poor woman forgetfully overdosing on her own heart medication, gave you the idea to have your uncle suffer a *similar* fate."

"Why," Brenda asked, "would I want that? I loved my uncle."

"Perhaps. But you probably loved him less after he discovered that you'd been selling antiques from the museum, replacing them with replicas Fred had made. Or perhaps this was just a suspicion of Barclay's that you knew would lead him to such a discovery. By the way, very clever of you, dear, to cast aspersions on your uncle for the unauthorized mishandling of antiques from this museum. Anyway, you put a fatal dosage of his medication in his favorite brand of beer, and once again solicited Fred Hackney's help, this time to make sure your uncle won that particular bottle at the raffle."

Brenda was shaking her head. "Everyone there saw how upset I was. I'm no actress, Mrs. Borne. I'm not like you — I can't fake tears."

"Oh, I truly believe you *were* upset when your uncle drank that beer immediately. You wanted him to take the bottle home, as was the general practice in the Tombola doings, and partake of it later — *not* draw such a commotion. And certainly not forcing you to witness the results of what you'd done."

"Is that right?" Brenda said with a smirk.

"And it was cunning of you to then throw suspicion on the other trustees, and for that I commend you. How would you say I'm doing so far?"

Brenda laughed behind closed lips. Then she said, "It's your show, Mrs. Borne. But isn't it always?"

Mother ignored the rhetorical question. "Then Fred Hackney began to give you problems — helping his loving if secret girlfriend pilfer antiques was one thing. . . . He may have taken pride in the quality of his replacement items, or otherwise, he would not have signed his work. But Fred be a knowing party to murder? That's another thing entirely. I doubt he even knew your uncle was supposed to die. Ah! I can see by your face that he didn't."

"Can you?"

"Poor Fred must have complained bitterly about being duped as he drove you to the hospital in Serenity, thereby effectively sealing his own fate. I would imagine he was very much in love with you, wasn't he, dear? He would *have* to have been, to do what he did."

Brenda seemed almost bored. "So you say. But why don't you try to find someone who saw us together, Mrs. Borne?"

"Oh, I'll leave that drudge work to the deputies. Where was I? Oh, yes. At our performance, after the lights went down, you sneaked backstage and made use of the tunnel — *yes,* dear, we found the tunnels, and we found Chad, too, where you left him. But I'll get to that."

"Get to it now."

"In due time. Where did I leave off? Oh, yes, you climbed the scaffolding, took Fred by surprise, pushed the poor man to his death, then returned to the theater just as the play was ending."

Mother paused for a breath, and I put in, "No wonder your comments didn't reflect the comic turn our performance took! At the time, when you said your uncle would have loved what we did to his favorite play, I was doubtful. You didn't see enough of the play to know what we'd done to it!"

Brenda shrugged. "Perhaps I don't have a sense of humor. Maybe I took what you did at face value, and was just being . . . nice."

"You being 'nice,' " Mother said, "seems to me terribly out of character right now. For example — perhaps you'd be so good as to tell me — what had Chad done to deserve your rancor? Had he discovered your pilfering? No? Had he spotted you putting the poisoned bottle on the raffle table? No?"

Brenda said, "So you haven't figured everything out to your satisfaction."

Mother's eyes flared with epiphany. "Wait, I think I have it. Chad must have noticed you going backstage and followed you through the tunnel. I can see by your expression, my dear, that *that* is exactly what happened! When you eventually stand trial, you will simply have to work up a better poker face."

"You need to work up a better reason for me supposedly killing Chad."

"How about this? Chad wanted money for his silence. So you set a meeting in the tunnel, and for protection, he brought what you thought was a gun, so you silenced him for good — then made it look as if he'd left town."

I said, "It was *you* driving Chad's car, loaded down with his belongings, who tried to run us down!"

Brenda's features were placid, expressionless. Had she not been so plain, that face of hers might have made a worthy cameo for the museum.

Finally she said, "Quite a story, Mrs. Borne. It has its wild elements, but someone might take it seriously. It's too bad for you that no one else will hear it."

Grimacing, she fired the pistol at Mother, point blank.

There was a *flash.*

A *bang.*

And a scream.

The scream did not come from Mother, or from me, rather Brenda herself as the antique pistol backfired, exploding in her hand, barrels peeling back like a blossom as a flower of red and orange and blue emerged and hung in the air before dissolving.

Mother and I stood there, momentarily stunned, then she expressed what I was thinking, "Well, *that* was certainly a piece of luck."

Brenda had dropped to her knees, the dress around her like a cake that had fallen. She was clutching the wrist of a hand that was a terrible gushing scarlet thing to see.

"Dear," Mother went on, "we'd best apply a tourniquet or the woman will bleed to death."

By "we" she meant me, and I went to the whimpering Brenda, ripped a sleeve from the dress — the ancient fabric tearing easily — and wrapped it tightly around her arm just below the elbow.

I had just finished tying the makeshift tourniquet when Sushi came running into the room, followed by an out-of-breath Sheriff Rudder. Lassie hadn't quite saved Timmy, but at least she'd brought the authorities.

Sushi, noting that Mother and I were all right, started barking at the wounded Brenda, but I silenced her with a single, "No!" No need to be smug about it. We had won, thanks to the volatility of ancient gunpowder.

Rudder demanded, "What happened here?"

"All in good time, Sheriff," Mother replied archly. "Right now, I suggest you summon the paramedics for this poor soul. In this instance, unless you are extremely sluggish in your response time, calling the EMTs would not be a waste of county resources."

A Trash 'n' Treasures Tip

Special caution should be used when firing antique guns containing old ammunition because they might explode and cause serious injury. Do I need to provide an example?

CHAPTER TWELVE:
ALL'S WELL THAT ENDS WELL?

After a sedated Brenda, in the company of a deputy, had been transported by ambulance to the hospital in nearby Selby, Sheriff Rudder himself wanted a brief accounting from Mother and me of what had happened. We sat in the museum's parlor and did so.

Rudder pulled over a Chippendale chair while we sat on a not-so-comfortable Victorian couch with walnut-carved back, Sushi on my lap.

"All right," he began. "Who wants to fill me in?"

Naturally, I deferred to Mother.

"Starting at what time, Sheriff?" she asked. "So much has happened today."

Rudder closed his eyes and sighed. "Start anywhere you like, Vivian."

"Very well." Mother took a deep breath. "This morning I went to church by myself — Brandy didn't, because she wanted to sleep in. There was difficulty in getting just the right seat in just the right pew, in order to properly surveil the suspects. But Father Cumberbatch was quite understanding, and his sermon, what I heard of it before dropping off, was quite compelling. Then after the service, I had the most delightful lunch with the Juliets. They're a group of local Old York women who meet every —"

"Mrs. Borne, please," he interrupted, touching his forehead as if taking his own temperature. "Only what's pertinent to the death of Chad Marlowe, and the injury of Brenda Starkadder. You'll both give formal statements later at the station. For now, anyway, I beg you to be succinct."

Mother drew herself up. "Well, beg all you like, but that just won't do! I must lead up to those two events, to create the proper context, to set the stage, so to speak. A bare stage, after all, is an empty, useless thing — one exception, of course, being my unique rendition of" — she leaned forward and whispered — "the Scottish play."

The sheriff's weary eyes looked pleadingly at me.

Helping him out, I said quickly, "Mother and I went to the theater around noon to get our check from Chad, but he wasn't there, and it looked like he'd skipped town.

Sushi led us to a door backstage that took us down into a tunnel where we found Chad's stabbed body. We called you and, while we were waiting, followed the tunnel to the museum, where Mother discovered that Brenda Starkadder, with Fred Hackney's help, had been substituting antiques for fakes. Brenda overheard us discussing this, and tried to silence us with an old gun, but the pistol backfired. The end." I raised my eyebrows — *succinct enough?*

Rudder's jaw muscles tightened. "All right, that will do for now. Be in my office first thing Monday morning."

Mother frowned. "But I have something *else* of importance to tell you about *today,* something Brandy wasn't privy to."

I glanced at her. What could that be? We'd never been separated throughout the ordeal.

He shook his head as he stood. "It'll keep till Monday morning."

She rose and gave him a half smile and half nod. "All right, my good man, if that's the way you want it. I merely thought you might want to listen to a certain recording I made. . . . Come, Brandy."

Mother took a step toward the parlor door, but Rudder stopped her with a traffic-cop hand. "*What* recording that you made?"

That's what I wanted to know!

306

She gave him a smug smile. "I recorded the entire confrontation with Brenda on my cell phone. Of course, the sound quality is a little iffy because it was in my pocket, but I'm sure any crack technician will be able to enhance it. You can send it to Des Moines or wherever the real detectives work."

Rudder burned at that remark while I looked up at Mother in surprise. "How did you manage that, while you were holding on to the fake tea box?"

Mother glanced down at me on the couch, where I still sat; Sushi stared up at her, as if she too would like an answer.

"Dear, neither holding on to a tea box nor secretly recording a conversation takes two hands. As soon as I spotted Brenda, I got that phone recording."

Rudder, forcing himself to be conciliatory, asked her, "May I have that cell, please?"

"Most certainly. Everything's there, Sheriff — explanations of all the murders, and Brenda's part in them, and her confession. Plenty to put her away for a good long while!" She produced it from her right slacks pocket and presented it to him like a medal he'd won.

Rudder, taking the cell, said, "Thank you, Vivian. This could prove helpful."

"You're quite welcome," Mother replied

magnanimously. Was that her faux Brit accent creeping in?

A female deputy stepped into the room. "Sheriff, forensics is here."

Rudder gave her a nod.

Mother raised a forefinger. "Might I make a small suggestion? Your CSI team should check the knives in the museum's weapons room as a possible source for the instrument used on Chad — in light of the antique pistol Brenda tried to use on us. She may have wiped it clean and put it back. Might I suggest spraying any possibilities with luminol, for examination under UV light?"

I would swear I could *hear* Rudder cringe.

Mother's forefinger remained aloft. "And one more thing. . . . I left my purse at the theater, Sheriff. I know the forensics men will be there soon, so why don't I just tiptoe backstage and snag it before I'm in the way?"

Shaking his head, he said, with a singsong sweetness that wasn't any more fake than a plastic rock with your house key in it, "Someone will bring your purse around to you at the inn within the hour. Is that satisfactory?"

"Quite," she said.

"Good-bye now."

"Good-bye!"

Mother, like any seasoned actor, knew when to exit, and we did. I was watching her closely because the only time she was more keyed up than after a stage performance was at the conclusion of a murder investigation. No pharmaceutical lab on earth could ever come up with a drug to tamp down this mood of Mother's.

Speaking of keyed up, when we returned to the inn, an unusually animated Seabert bounded up to us as we stepped into the small lobby.

"Is it true that Chad Marlowe is dead," he said in a rush, "and that Brenda is the prime suspect?"

"Yes," Mother said, but before she could elaborate, her mouth hanging open in midair, Seabert turned his back and got on his cell phone.

"Celia," he said, "Mrs. Borne has confirmed the rumor. . . . Yes, absolutely. . . . When will the meeting be over? . . . All right."

He clicked off the cell and turned back to us with an obsequious smile. "Sorry. Does this mean you dear ladies will be staying another night?"

"What meeting?" Mother demanded, ignoring the innkeeper's query.

"Oh. Well. The trustees have gathered for an emergency meeting at the Community Center."

She frowned. "In order to pass incorporation?"

"Uh, yes. That's right."

I said to him, "Because Chad and Brenda are out of the picture now?"

"Well, yes. But surely you understand that it's the right way to go, that it's what Old York so desperately needs."

Mother said, "Mr. Falwell, in all things, there's a right way and a wrong way. But there's also a third way. The Vivian Borne way. Come, Brandy."

"No. First let me deposit Sushi in our room. She needs a nap. She's had a busier day than we have."

"Agreed. But make haste."

I made it, and soon Mother and I were cutting straight across the village green to the Community Center.

"What's the Vivian Borne way?" I asked her, as we strode briskly along. "I mean, I know there's *always* a Vivian Borne way, but what is it in this instance?"

"Dear, we — that is, *I* — must make an impassioned plea."

She elucidated no further.

But I didn't have long to wait. When we

310

arrived, Mother went over and planted herself in front of them — Celia, Digby, Father Cumberbatch, and Flora, all seated at their regular board-meeting table.

She asked, "Have you put the incorporation issue to a vote yet?"

They exchanged glances, and then the priest said, "We were just about to, Mrs. Borne."

"Might I have a word before you do?"

Digby said, "We're having a meeting here, lady. You're not a trustee, in fact you're not even an Old York resident. I for one have heard more than enough of your opinions, and I think you should leave."

But the others were shaking their heads, saying, "No," and "Let her speak."

Celia said, "As temporary chair, I recognize Vivian Borne. If you have something to say, Mrs. Borne, say it. I feel you've earned the right."

"I believe I have, Mrs. Falwell. This board surely owes me some consideration for revealing the truth about these deaths — one accidental, and three that were cold-blooded murders — and in so doing removing any suspicion from the board's collective doorstep . . . and your personal ones."

I was sitting where I had before, by the way, when I'd been taking notes on Tony's interrogation of the trustees and other Tombola suspects.

They exchanged looks.

Then spokeswoman Celia said, "All right, Mrs. Borne. But you're not going to change anyone's vote, if that's why you're here. And right now we stand three to one."

"Oh, I don't intend on changing anyone's vote," Mother replied, garnering puzzled expressions from the group. "I fully expect the vote to be as you say."

"Then I don't get what you want," Digby said.

Mother looked at him sadly. "I'm afraid you really don't, Mr. Lancaster."

"Huh?"

"*Get* it. You see, it is possible to bring Old York into the twenty-first century without spoiling its quaint, Old English charm. But not by bringing in a tacky strip mall whose shops bear tasteless sobriquets — Ye Olde Laundromat indeed."

Celia, seated next to Digby, swiveled to him. "Is *that* what you're planning on doing?"

Father Cumberbatch, on the other side of the land developer, reared back to look at him. "That's not the kind of thing *I'd* like to see, Digby."

"Me, either," Flora said brightly, her lone

312

"no" vote giving her some hope.

Digby spread his hands. "Hey, I thought the majority of us wanted the same thing — *change*!"

And the four began arguing, talking over each other, getting nowhere.

Mother placed a finger and thumb in her mouth and blew an eardrum-rattling whistle. My ears were already covered.

"I do in fact have a suggestion," she said, filling the startled silence. "If you care to hear it."

Bewildered shrugs all around.

"By all means, good people, pass incorporation. But have your new city ordinance, or building code, or zoning regulations, *whatever*, define and limit the type of businesses that can occupy space around the village green and within town limits. That way, the quaintness of Old York — which brings in tourist trade, after all — can be preserved. No new business can open without board of trustees approval."

Digby started to protest, but Mother raised a finger. "You *can* have your strip mall, Mr. Lancaster . . . but on the outskirts of town."

Everyone waited for Digby's response.

Finally he spoke. "I guess I could live with that. My undeveloped land *is* on the outskirts, but I do own some buildings around the square, and I'm not wild about being told what I can or can't do with them." He paused thoughtfully. "However, I can see the profitability in limiting what goes into those buildings. In maintaining a certain look and image for the town, and building the tourist trade."

Mother smiled at him. "I thought I could count on your common sense, Mr. Lancaster — when it's spelled c-e-n-t-s, at least."

That brought a few chuckles from the others.

Mother then addressed Flora. "As for you, dear, you shouldn't be afraid of a little competition. People get complacent without it. Competition makes one try harder. And, to be frank, your flowers *are* overpriced. But perhaps you can convince the board not to approve a similar business when the town already has one."

Celia cleared her throat. "Ah . . . thank you, Mrs. Borne. We'll consider your suggestion of restricted businesses, around the green especially."

But Mother wasn't about to be shuffled off the stage just yet. "I have one other small suggestion, which just came to me."

"Yes?" Celia prompted.

"That you have me perform each year at

your fete."

Just came to her?

"The audience's enthusiastic response to my one-woman show — *two*-woman, including my hat handler — indicates that an annual performance would be something looked forward to by one and all. And each year I would bring some new delight to life. For example, I am mulling a bang-up condensation of *Hamlet* in which I play all the parts, wearing different shoes."

They were staring at her like Martians regarding Mount Rushmore.

I rushed forward and took Mother's arm.

"Thank you for hearing us out," I said to the trustees. "Mother's offer is something you should obviously discuss among yourselves." I turned to Mother: "I think it's time we left, and let the board get on with its vote."

"Of *course,* dear," she replied. She gave them a smile and a half bow.

As we turned to leave, Mother looked back at them and made the forefinger and thumb gesture signifying, "Call me."

Monday morning, Mother and I were back in Serenity, seated in Sheriff Rudder's office in the county jail downtown.

The big lawman in the tan uniform sat at

315

a cluttered metal desk, having called us in for what I assumed to be a more detailed debriefing, and probably a (grudging) pat on our backs for solving the murders of Barclay, Fred, and Chad, and clearing up Millie's death as accidental.

When we'd finished giving our official statements, Mother asked, "How's Brenda doing?"

"She's in the maximum security wing of a hospital in Iowa City," the sheriff replied. "Never mind which one."

"Not *where,* dear. I have no particular interest in visiting her. *How* is she doing?"

Rudder seemed to be working at not looking annoyed. "She's missing three fingers, Vivian. She'll never play piano again."

"Why, did she? Play the piano?"

I said, "I think the sheriff is being droll, Mother."

"Oh," Mother said. To Rudder, she said, "Were they able to be sewn back on, the fingers?"

"No, Vivian. They were quite mangled."

"That's terrible."

"Yes, it is."

"They'd have been useful for fingerprint analysis."

Rudder's jaw tightened and a vein in his temple began to throb. "I appreciate you

316

pointing that out, Vivian. I begin to wonder how we managed around here before you . . . took an interest."

"You're welcome. Go on — do please continue, re: Brenda's state of health."

The sheriff shifted in his chair. "Well, she's in stable condition, but might well have died if it hadn't been for Brandy's quick action in applying a tourniquet." He said to me, "You're to be commended."

"Thanks," I said. "But it was a team effort."

"Then the woman will be able to stand trial?" Mother asked, finally revealing her true concern.

Rudder's ruddy face reddened further, and he leaned forward, his words clipped. "Do the two of you realize . . . do you even *know* . . . how badly you've compromised every one of the crime scenes?" His eyes had been on her, but then they landed on me.

"She did it," I blurted, pointing a thumb at her.

Mother shot me a sideways glance. "So much for team effort!"

Rudder raised a hand. "*Whoever* was responsible, evidence was severely weakened."

Pats on the back, not so much. Dressing

down? Oh yes.

"Picky, picky, picky," Mother said. "Evidence *abounds* to convict that woman! Isn't it enough that I — *we* — handed you the killer? Must we *convict* her, too? Must we do *everyone's* job?" She took a deep breath and pressed fearlessly on. "Why, if we hadn't conducted our own investigation into these deaths, they would still be listed as accidental. Except, of course, for Chad. *That* one was obvious. It's unlikely he fell on a knife, after all. And, of course, Millie almost certainly accidentally overdosed herself. But Barclay and Fred . . . *puh-leeze!*"

Rudder raised his palms. "Okay, Vivian, crawl down off your high horse. All I'm saying is that the way you went about things, particularly at crime scenes, hasn't exactly made putting together our case against Brenda Starkadder an easy one."

Mother's chin rose. "Apology accepted."

"Uh, that wasn't anything *like* an apology, Vivian. *Your* fingerprints were found on everything from the scaffolding at the church to the wastebasket in Chad's apartment, and of course the tunnel doors. And must I mention how many laws the two of you broke conducting your unofficial investigation? Admittedly, they're misdemeanors, but they still muddy our waters."

Mother squirmed in her chair. "Very well, I concede we may have taken a few liberties, here and there — mind you, we're not admitting anything, I'm not under oath — and, yes, I may have been a teensy-weensy bit careless in regard to touching things."

"Sheriff," I said, starting to get riled, "that evil woman tried to *kill* us."

Rudder gave me an arched eyebrow. "Did she? Or was Brenda protecting herself and the museum from burglars? You *did* technically break in."

Mother's eyebrows rose above her big glasses. "Is *that* what she's saying?"

Rudder nodded. "That's what she's saying."

I asked, "And you believe her?"

"No. She's guilty as sin." The sheriff shrugged. "But the question is — what will a jury think?"

Mother was frowning. "It won't be helpful when she holds up that mutilated hand getting sworn in." She leaned forward. "What about Chad's blue Mustang? Have you found it?"

"Yes. In Brenda's garage at her home. She hadn't had a chance to dispose of it yet. That's damning evidence in itself."

"Loaded down with his things, right?" I asked, adding, "She wanted it to look like he'd left town."

The sheriff sat back. "Brenda claims Chad *was* leaving town, and asked her to store his car and possessions so they wouldn't get stolen overnight." He spread his hands. "Who knows what a good defense lawyer might pull off for a client this devious?"

Mother and I exchanged alarmed glances.

Then Mother asked, "I don't know what all this fuss is about. You have her confession on my cell phone recording. What more could the county attorney desire? You should have her dead to rights!"

"Reminds me," Rudder said.

He opened a drawer, put Mother's cell phone on the desk, and pushed it toward her.

Then he said, "No confession on there, Vivian. It's all your own conjecture. Brenda says very little. Oh, I'm not saying it's not helpful hearing your speculation on how Brenda might have killed these people."

"*Might* have?" I said. "What about the knife used on Chad?"

He didn't answer immediately. It appeared he was considering whether he should share certain information.

Then: "We did find a knife in the museum weapons room that showed traces of blood on the blade, along with Brenda's prints."

"Matching her remaining fingers, I trust," Mother said.

"Yes, Vivian. Matching her remaining fingers."

"Then she'll be charged for Chad's death, at least," I said.

"I think I can safely say yes to that. And right now, that's all you two are going to get from me." He pushed back his chair and stood.

Clearly we'd been dismissed.

But at least Rudder did us the courtesy of walking us out of the office and buzzing us through a security door into the outer area.

In the jail's modern lobby, which might be mistaken for any airport-gate waiting area, Mother and I stood facing each other. No one else was around, other than a deputy busy behind a Plexiglas window.

Hands on hips, I chided, "I hope you've learned your lesson."

"What lesson is that, dear?"

"About not contaminating a crime scene!"

Nodding solemnly, Mother replied, "I certainly have. In future, we will both be sure to wear latex gloves, and possibly even those cute little blue booties. We'll look online to see where to purchase them!"

That night I was back at Tony's cabin. It

seemed like eons ago that Mother had flounced in on us to announce we were going to Old York . . . but it had only been five days.

Outside, it was chilly and rainy, but inside Tony had a fire going, making the cabin nice and cozy. He had promised to cook his famous lasagna (famous to me), so I was looking forward to this evening.

But first, I knew I would have to endure the inevitable lecture, which occurred shortly after Sushi and I arrived.

"You know," Tony said sternly, "you could have been killed."

We were seated on the couch in front of the snap, crackle, popping fireplace; Sushi and Rocky lay on the rug enjoying the warmth of the flames, like an old if unlikely married couple.

"I know," I said. "We were really stupid."

"If that gun hadn't misfired . . ." He shook his head. "I don't even want to think about it."

"We were lucky," I admitted.

Funny how you can be honestly contrite yet still resent a lecture. He was right, of course he was right, but we *had* brought a very dangerous murderess to justice. Assuming we hadn't contaminated those crime scenes *too* badly . . .

Tony was saying, "I wish you could control that woman."

Mother. But you knew that.

"I *do* try, Tony. But if I refuse her, she goes ahead without me."

"Well, let her."

I twisted toward him. "It doesn't work that way. Because of her bipolar disorder, I feel a responsibility to keep an eye on her."

"And what about your responsibility to us?"

And there it was. Other men in my life had found out the hard way that my loyalty, first and foremost, was to Mother. Did Tony and I have to face that nasty reality right now?

"Look, sweetie," I said, "our TV show will start filming in a few weeks, and that will keep Mother plenty busy."

Tony nodded, even smiled a little. "Good to hear. What's the production schedule?"

I sighed. "Pretty hectic, since they'll be shooting all the episodes back to back. And we'll be busy with a lot of preproduction stuff. I'm not sure how much time you and I will have together for a while."

And maybe a slight breather from each other wouldn't be the worst thing ever. Though it sounded like it.

Tony slipped an arm around my shoulders

and pulled me to him. "Understood. Just give me a call whenever you come up for air."

We kissed. Both Sushi and Rocky came over, nudging their noses at us.

"They're not jealous," Tony said. "They want lasagna."

"So does Brandy," I laughed.

TONY'S LASAGNA

1 lb. Italian sausage
1 clove garlic, minced
1 tbl. basil
1 1/2 tsp. salt
2 cups diced tomatoes (1-pound can)
1 1/3 cups tomato paste (12-ounce can)
10 ounces lasagna noodles
3 cups ricotta
1/2 cup grated Parmesan cheese
2 tbl. parsley
2 beaten eggs
1 tsp. salt
1/2 tsp. pepper
1 lb. mozzarella cheese, sliced thin

Brown sausage; drain. Add garlic, basil, salt, tomatoes, and tomato paste. Simmer, uncovered, 30 minutes, stirring occasionally.

Cook noodles in boiling water until tender; drain; rinse.

In a bowl combine ricotta, Parmesan cheese, parsley, beaten eggs, salt, and pepper.

In a 13-by-9-by-2-inch greased baking dish, spread half the noodles on the bottom; next, half the ricotta cheese mixture; half the mozarella cheese; and half the meat sauce. Repeat layers. Bake at 375 degrees for about 30 minutes. Let stand 5 minutes before cutting into squares. Serves about 8 to 10 people.

Tony was in the kitchen assembling the lasagna layers in a pan — the dogs watching closely for any dropped morsels — and I was in the outer room, setting the table, when a knock came at the door.

"I'll get it," I called. I knew it wasn't Mother, because she was with her gal pals at a meeting of her mystery book club, the Red-Hatted League. Fittingly, they were reading and discussing *Too Many Cooks,* by Rex Stout.

Still, a hit man had once come figuratively knocking here, so I checked the peephole.

It was a woman I didn't recognize.

I opened the door, keeping the screen between us.

"Yes?" I said.

About fifty, tall and slender, with dark hair, olive skin, and deep-set eyes, she was dressed tastefully, if not expensively, in a beige sweater, black tailored slacks, and patent-leather flats. The purse hanging from one shoulder was Burberry plaid.

"I need to see Anthony."

"Tony's rather busy at the moment," I said pleasantly. "Can I tell him what this is about?"

She said, not at all pleasantly, "No. I'll tell him myself."

"Okay. Well, who should I say you are?"

Her chin jutted up. "*Mrs.* Anthony Cassato. His wife."

To be continued . . .

A TRASH 'N' TREASURES TIP

When purchasing a foreign antique as an investment, keep in mind that it might not be desirable in your own country. Mother and I have a Bohemian cuckoo clock in our store we can't seem to give away. If you're looking for a clock of that kind, what I meant to say was, it's available at a fair price.

ABOUT THE AUTHORS

Barbara Allan is a joint pseudonym of husband-and-wife mystery writers Barbara and Max Allan Collins.

Barbara Collins is a highly respected short story writer in the mystery field, with appearances in over a dozen top anthologies, including *Murder Most Delicious, Women on the Edge, Deadly Housewives,* and the best-selling *Cat Crimes* series. She was the coeditor of (and a contributor to) the best-selling anthology *Lethal Ladies,* and her stories were selected for inclusion in the first three volumes of *The Year's 25 Finest Crime and Mystery Stories.*

Two acclaimed hardcover collections of her work have been published — *Too Many Tomcats* and (with her husband) *Murder — His and Hers.* The Collinses' first novel together, the baby boomer thriller *Regeneration,* was a paperback best-seller; their second collaborative novel, *Bombshell* — in which Marilyn Monroe saves the world from World War III — was published in hardcover to excellent reviews. Both are back in print under the "Barbara Allan" byline.

Barbara also has been the production manager and/or line producer on several independent film projects.

Max Allan Collins has been hailed as "the Renaissance man of mystery fiction." He has earned an unprecedented twenty-two Private Eye Writers of America "Shamus" nominations for his Nathan Heller historical thrillers, winning for *True Detective* (1983) and *Stolen Away* (1991).

His other credits include film criticism, short fiction, songwriting, trading-card sets, and movie/TV tie-in novels, including the *New York Times* best-sellers *Saving Private Ryan* and the Scribe Award–winning *American Gangster.*

His graphic novel *Road to Perdition,* considered a classic of the form, is the basis of the Academy Award–winning film. Max's other comics credits include the "Dick Tracy" syndicated strip; his own "Ms. Tree"; "Batman"; and "CSI: Crime Scene Investigation," based on the hit TV series, for which he also wrote six video games and ten best-selling novels.

An acclaimed, award-winning filmmaker in the Midwest, he wrote and directed the Lifetime movie *Mommy* (1996) and three other features; his produced screenplays include the 1995 HBO World Premiere *The Expert* and *The Last Lullaby* (2008). His 1998 documentary *Mike Hammer's Mickey Spillane* appears on the Criterion Collection release of the acclaimed film noir, *Kiss Me Deadly.* The current Cinemax TV series *Quarry* is based on his innovative book series.

Max's most recent novels include two works begun by his mentor, the late mystery-writing legend Mickey Spillane: *Kill Me, Darling* (with Mike Hammer) and *The Legend of Caleb York,* the first western credit for both Spillane and Collins.

"Barbara Allan" lives in Muscatine, Iowa, their Serenity-esque hometown. Son Nathan works as a translator of Japanese to English, with credits ranging from video games to novels.

The employees of Thorndike Press hope you have enjoyed this Large Print book. All our Thorndike, Wheeler, and Kennebec Large Print titles are designed for easy reading, and all our books are made to last. Other Thorndike Press Large Print books are available at your library, through selected bookstores, or directly from us.

For information about titles, please call:
   (800) 223-1244

or visit our Web site at:
   http://gale.cengage.com/thorndike

To share your comments, please write:
   Publisher
   Thorndike Press
   10 Water St., Suite 310
   Waterville, ME 04901

4/17